"The South Won!"

The South Won, What If?

Colonel Cha W.

The history is correc., ~~~ the Optional
outcome is fictional.
Three missed opportunities could have
changed everything!
The South had at least three chances to win
the war.
What If?

ISBN 978-1-61364-921-3
Edited by, Larry P. Whitt

Published by Dahnmon Whitt Family
Post Office Box 831
Flatwoods, KY 41139
http://dahnmonwhittfamily.com

Contents

"What If"?

"Dahnmon Whitt Family Publishing"

Source: Wikipedia, the free encyclopedia

"The South Won"

The First Battle

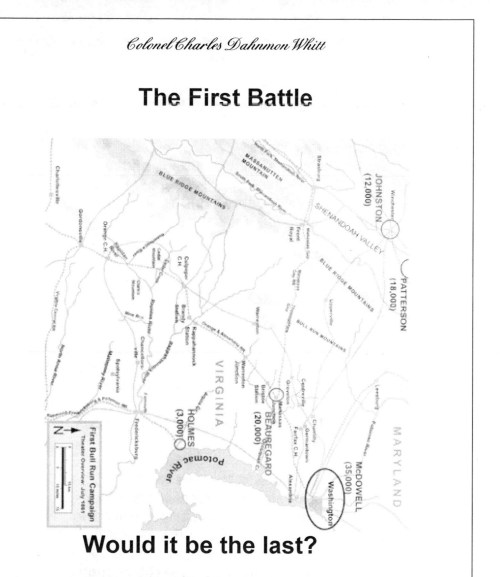

Would it be the last?

Northern Virginia Theater in July 1861

Further information from the Map:
Confederate order of battle, battle Brig. Gen.
Irvin McDowell was appointed by President

"What If"?

Abraham Lincoln to command the Army of North-eastern Virginia.

Once in this capacity, McDowell was harassed by impatient politicians and citizens in Washington, who wished to see a quick battlefield victory over the Confederate Army in northern Virginia.

McDowell, however, was concerned about the untried nature of his army. He was reassured by President Lincoln, "You are green, it is true, but they are green also; you are all green alike." Against his better judgment, McDowell commenced campaigning. On July 16, 1861, the general departed Washington with the largest field army yet gathered on the North American continent, about 35,000 men (28,452 with guns)

McDowell's plan was to move westward in three columns, make a diversionary attack on the Confederate line at Bull Run with two columns, while the third column moved around the Confederates' right flank to the south, cutting off the railroad to Richmond and threatening the rear of the rebel army. He assumed that the Confederates would be forced to abandon Manassas Junction and fall back to the Rappahannock River, the next defensible line in Virginia, which would relieve some of the pressure on the U.S. capital.

The Confederate Army of the Potomac (21,883 with guns) under Beauregard was encamped near Manassas Junction, approximately 25 miles from the United States capital. McDowell planned to attack this numerically inferior enemy army. Union Maj. Gen. Robert Patterson's 18,000 men engaged Johnston's force (the Army of the Shenandoah at 8,884 effectives, augmented by Maj. Gen. Theophilus H. Holmes's brigade of 1,465 in the Shenandoah Valley, preventing them from reinforcing Beauregard.

After two days of marching slowly in the sweltering heat, the Union army was allowed to rest in Centreville. McDowell reduced the size of his army to approximately 30,000 by dispatching Brig. Gen. Theodore Runyon with 5,000 troops to protect the army's rear. In the meantime, McDowell searched for a way to outflank Beauregard, who had drawn up his lines along Bull Run. On July 18, the Union commander sent a division under Brig. Gen. Daniel Tyler to pass on the Confederate right (southeast) flank. Tyler was drawn into a skirmish at Blackburn's Ford over Bull Run and made no headway.

"What If"?

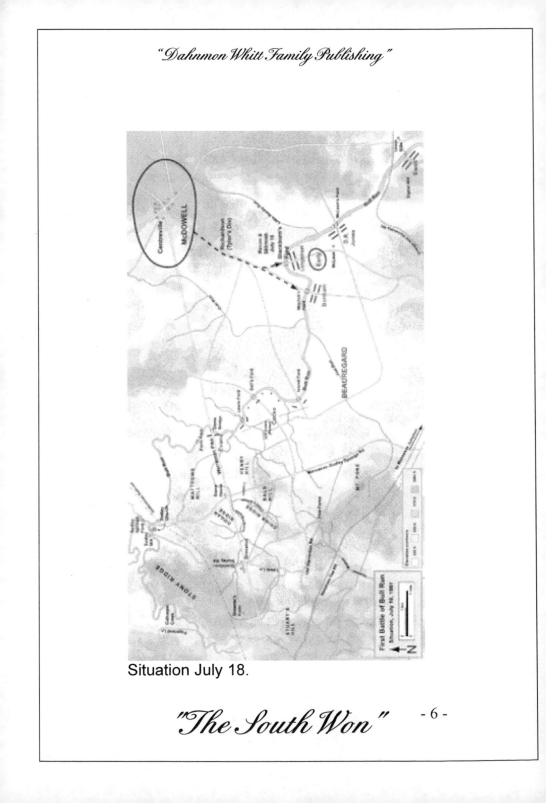

Situation July 18.

"The South Won" - 6 -

Becoming more frustrated, McDowell resolved to attack the Confederate left (northwest) flank instead. He planned to attack with Brig. Gen. Daniel Tyler's division at the Stone Bridge on the Warrenton Turnpike and send the divisions of Brig. Generals, David Hunter and Samuel P. Heintzelman over Sudley Springs Ford. From here, these divisions could march into the Confederate rear. The brigade of Col. Israel B. Richardson (Tyler's Division) would harass the enemy at Blackburn's Ford, preventing them from slowing the main attack. Patterson would tie down Johnston in the Shenandoah Valley so that reinforcements could not reach the area. Although McDowell had arrived at a theoretically sound plan, it had a number of flaws: it was one that required synchronized execution of troop movements and attacks, skills that had not been developed in the recent army; it relied on actions by Patterson that he had already failed to take; finally, McDowell had delayed long enough that Johnston's Valley force was able to board trains at Piedmont Station and rush to Manassas Junction to reinforce Beauregard's men.

On July 19–20, significant reinforcements bolstered the Confederate lines behind Bull Run.

"What If"?

Johnston arrived with all of his army, except for the troops of Brig. Gen. Kirby Smith, who were still in transit. Most of the new arrivals were posted in the vicinity of Blackburn's Ford and Beauregard's plan was to attack from there to the north toward Centreville. Johnston, the senior officer, approved the plan. If both of the armies had been able to execute their plans simultaneously, it would have resulted in a mutual counterclockwise movement as they attacked each other's left flank.

McDowell was getting contradictory information from his intelligence agents, so he called for the balloon *Enterprise*, which was being demonstrated by Prof. Thaddeus S. C. Lowe in Washington, to perform aerial reconnaissance.

Situation morning, July 21

"What If"?

On the morning of July 21, McDowell sent the divisions of Hunter and Heintzelman (about 12,000 men) from Centreville at 2:30 a.m., marching southwest on the Warrenton Turnpike and then turning northwest toward Sudley Springs. Tyler's division (about 8,000) marched directly toward the Stone Bridge. The inexperienced units immediately developed logistical problems. Tyler's division blocked the advance of the main flanking column on the turnpike. The latter units found the approach roads to Sudley Springs were inadequate, little more than a cart path in some places, and did not begin fording Bull Run until 9:30 a.m. Tyler's men reached the Stone Bridge around 6 a.m.

At 5:15 a.m., Richardson's brigade fired a few artillery rounds across Mitchell's Ford on

the Confederate right, some of which hit Beauregard's headquarters in the Wilmer McLean house as he was eating breakfast, alerting him to the fact that his offensive battle plan had been preempted. Nevertheless, he ordered   attacks north toward the Union left at Centreville. Bungled orders and poor communications prevented their execution. Although he intended for Brig. Gen. Richard S. Ewell to lead the attack, Ewell, at Union Mills Ford, was simply ordered to "hold ... in readiness to advance at a moment's notice." Brig. Gen. D.R. Jones was supposed to attack in support of Ewell, but found himself moving forward alone. Holmes was also supposed to support, but received no orders at all.

All that stood in the path of the 20,000 Union soldiers converging on the Confederate left flank were Col. Nathan "Shanks" Evans and his reduced brigade of 1,100 men. Evans had moved some of his men to intercept the direct threat from Tyler at the bridge, but he began to suspect that the weak attacks from the Union brigade of Brig. Gen. Robert C. Schenck were merely feints, (deception). He was informed of the main Union flanking movement through Sudley Springs by Captain Edward Porter Alexander,

"What If"?

Beauregard's signal officer, observing from 8 miles southwest on Signal Hill. In the first use of wig-wag semaphore signaling in combat, Alexander sent the *message "Look out for your left, your position is turned."* Shanks hastily led 900 of his men from their position fronting the Stone Bridge to a new location on the slopes of Matthews Hill, a low rise to the northwest of his previous position.

Evans soon received reinforcement from two other brigades under Brig. Gen. Barnard Bee and Col. Francis S. Bartow, bringing the force on the flank to 2,800 men. They successfully slowed Hunter's lead brigade (Brig. Gen. Ambrose E. Burnside) in its attempts to ford Bull Run and advance across Young's Branch, at the northern end of Henry House Hill. One of Tyler's brigade commanders, Col. William T. Sherman, crossed at an unguarded ford and struck the right flank of the Confederate defenders. This surprise attack, coupled with pressure from Burnside and Maj. George Sykes, collapsed the Confederate line shortly after 11:30 a.m., sending them in a disorderly retreat to Henry House Hill.

As they retreated from their Matthews Hill position, the remainder of Evans's, Bee's, and Bartow's commands received some cover from Capt. John D. Imboden and his battery of four 6-pounder guns, which held off the Union advance while the Confederates attempted to regroup on Henry House Hill. They were met by Generals Johnston and Beauregard, who had just arrived from Johnston's headquarters at the M. Lewis Farm. Fortunately for the Confederates, McDowell did not press his advantage and attempt to seize the strategic ground immediately, choosing to bombard the hill with the batteries of Captain's James B. Ricketts (Battery I, 1st U.S. Artillery) and Charles Griffin (Battery D, 5th U.S.) from Dogan's Ridge.

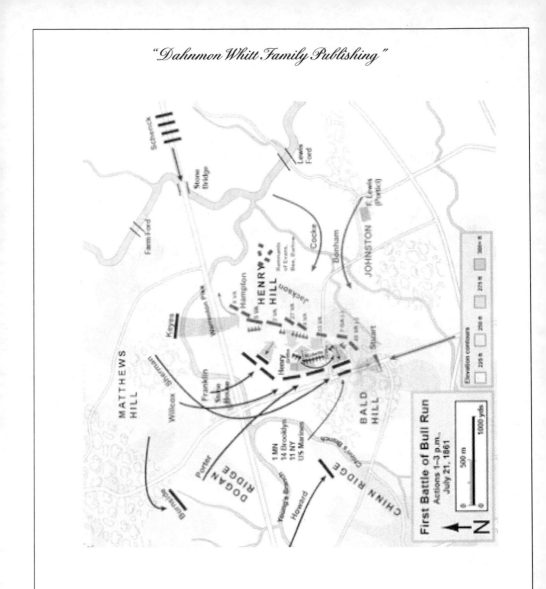

Attacks on Henry House Hill, noon–2 p.m.

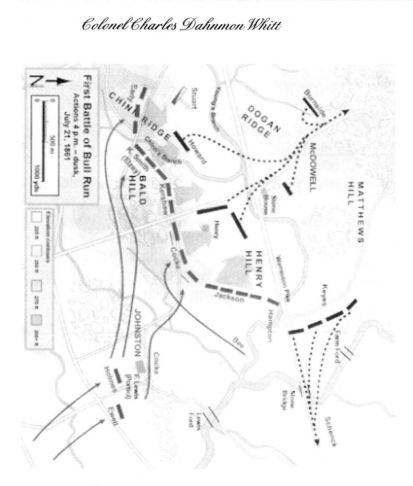

Union retreat, after 4 p.m.

Brig. Gen Thomas J. Jackson's Virginia brigade came up in support of the disorganized Confederates around noon, accompanied by Col. Wade Hampton and his Hampton's Legion, and Colonel J.E.B. Stuart's cavalry. Jackson posted his five regiments on the reverse slope of the hill, where they were shielded from direct fire,

"What If"?

and was able to assemble 13 guns for the defensive line, which he posted on the crest of the hill; <u>as the guns fired, their recoil moved them down the reverse slope, where they could be safely reloaded.</u>

Meanwhile, McDowell ordered the batteries of Ricketts and Griffin to move from Dogan's Ridge to the hill for close infantry support. Their 11 guns engaged in a fierce artillery duel across 300 yards against Jackson's 13. Unlike many engagements in the Civil War, here the Confederate artillery had an advantage.

The Union pieces were now within range of the Confederate smoothbores and the predominantly rifled pieces on the Union side were not effective weapons at such close ranges, with many shots fired over the head of their targets.

One of the casualties of the artillery fire was Judith Carter Henry, an 85-year-old widow and invalid, who was unable to leave her bedroom in the Henry House. As Ricketts began receiving rifle fire, he concluded that it was coming from the Henry House and turned his guns on the building. A shell that crashed through the bedroom wall tore off one of the widow's feet and inflicted multiple injuries, from which she died later that day

Ruins of Judith Henry's house, "Spring Hill", after the battle

"The Enemy are driving us "," Bee exclaimed to Jackson. Jackson, a former U.S. Army officer and professor at the Virginia Military Institute, is said to have replied, "Then, Sir, we will give them the bayonet." Bee exhorted his own troops to re-form by shouting, *"There is Jackson standing like a stone wall. Let us determine to die here, and we will conquer. Rally behind the Virginians."* There is some controversy over Bee's statement

"What If"?

and intent, which could not be clarified because he was mortally wounded almost immediately after speaking and none of his subordinate officers wrote reports of the battle. Major Burnett Rhett, chief of staff to General Johnston, claimed that Bee was angry at Jackson's failure to come immediately to the relief of Bee's and Bartow's brigades while they were under heavy pressure. Those who subscribe to this opinion believe that Bee's statement was meant to belittle Jackson: *Look at Jackson standing there like a stone wall!"*

Artillery commander Griffin decided to move two of his guns to the southern end of his line, hoping to provide concealed fire against the Confederates. At approximately 3 p.m., these guns were overrun by the 33rd Virginia, whose men were outfitted in blue uniforms, causing Griffin's commander, Maj. William F. Barry, to mistake them for Union troops and to order Griffin not to fire on them. Close range volleys from the 33rd Virginia and Stuart's cavalry attack against the flank of the 11th New York Volunteer Infantry Regiment (Ellsworth's Fire Zouaves), which was supporting the battery, killed many of the gunners and scattered the infantry. Capitalizing on this success, Jackson ordered two regiments to charge Ricketts's guns and they were captured as well. As additional Federal infantry engaged, the guns changed hands several times.

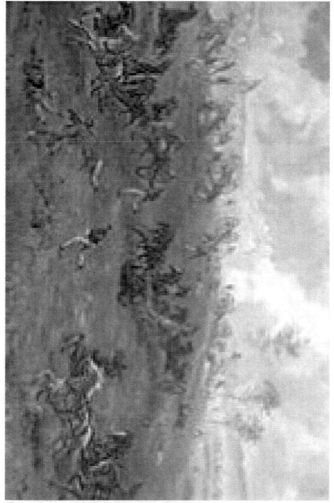

Capture of Ricketts' Battery,

The capture of the Union guns turned the tide of battle. Although McDowell had brought 15 regiments into the fight on the hill, outnumbering the Confederates two to one, no more than two were ever engaged simultaneously. Jackson continued to press his attacks, telling soldiers of the 4th Virginia Infantry, "*Reserve your fire until they come within 50 yards! Then fire and give them the bayonet! And when you charge, yell like furies!*" For the first time, Union troops heard the disturbing sound of the Rebel yell. At about 4 p.m., the last Union troops were pushed off Henry House Hill by a charge of two regiments from Col. Philip St. George Cocke's brigade.

To the west, Chinn Ridge had been occupied by Col. Oliver O. Howard's brigade from Heintzelman's division. Also at 4 p.m., two Confederate brigades that had just arrived from the Shenandoah Valley—Col. Jubal A. Early's and Brig. Gen. Kirby Smith's (commanded by Col. Arnold Elzey after Smith was wounded)—crushed Howard's brigade. Beauregard ordered his entire line forward. McDowell's force crumbled and began to retreat.

The retreat was relatively orderly up to the Bull Run crossings, but it was poorly managed by the Union officers. A Union wagon was overturned by artillery fire on a bridge spanning Cub Run Creek and incited panic in McDowell's force. As the soldiers streamed uncontrollably toward Centreville, discarding their arms and equipment,

McDowell ordered Col. Dixon S. Miles's division to act as a rear guard, but it was impossible to rally the army short of Washington. In the disorder that followed, hundreds of Union troops were taken prisoner. Expecting an easy Union victory, the wealthy elite of nearby Washington, including congressmen and their families, had come to picnic and watch the battle. When the Union army was driven back in a running disorder, the roads back to Washington were blocked by panicked civilians attempting to flee in their carriages.

Since their combined army had been left highly disorganized as well, Beauregard and Johnston did not fully press their advantage, despite urging from Confederate President Jefferson Davis, who had arrived on the battlefield to see the Union soldiers retreating. An attempt by Johnston to intercept the Union troops from his right flank, using the brigades of Brig. Gens. Milledge L. Bonham and James Longstreet, was a failure. The two commanders squabbled with each other and when

"What If"? - 21 -

Bonham's men received some artillery fire from the Union rear guard, and found that Richardson's brigade blocked the road to Centreville, he called off the pursuit.

Aftermath of the Battle

Today will be known as BLACK MONDAY, To the Union.

"We are utterly and disgracefully routed, beaten, whipped by secessionists."

Union diary keeper, George Templeton Strong

"If the war had turned out to be of short duration, Bull Run would have been a disaster for the Union. But if, as now seemed more plausible, a long and nasty war was inevitable, that battle had a curiously salutary effect for the Union side. It provided a wake-up call for those optimists, like Seward or even Lincoln, who had hoped for or counted on a quick result."

David Detzer, *Donnybrook*

Manassas was a turning point in the American Civil War; in the sense that the battle struck with impelling force upon public opinion at home and abroad, upon

Congress, and upon the Commander-in-chief. It framed new patterns of thought and led to far-reaching changes in the conduct of the war. The failure at Bull Run inspired a second Northern rising. Volunteering accelerated, 90-day men reenlisted, and States rushed fresh regiments forward in large numbers. As they realized victory would not come readily, a new mood fastened upon Northerners. An iron resolve entered the Northern soul.

James A. Rawley, *Turning Points of the Civil War*

Bull Run was the largest and bloodiest battle in American history up to that point. Union casualties were 460 killed, 1,124 wounded, and 1,312 missing or captured; Confederate casualties were 387 killed, 1,582 wounded, and 13 missing. Among the latter was Col. Francis S. Bartow, who was the first Confederate brigade commander to be killed in the Civil War. General Bee was mortally wounded and died the following day.

<u>Union forces and civilians alike feared that Confederate forces would advance on Washington, D.C., with very little standing in their way.</u> On July 24, Prof. Thaddeus S. C. Lowe ascended in the balloon *Enterprise* to observe the Confederates moving in and

"What If"?

about Manassas Junction and Fairfax. He saw no evidence of massing Rebel forces, but was forced to land in Confederate territory. It was overnight before he was rescued and could report to headquarters. He reported that his observations "restored confidence" to the Union commanders.

The Northern public was shocked at the unexpected defeat of their army when an easy victory had been widely anticipated. Both sides quickly came to realize the war would be longer and more brutal than they had imagined. On July 22 President Lincoln signed a bill that provided for the enlistment of another 500,000 men for up to three years of service.

The reaction in the Confederacy was more muted. There was little public celebration as the Southerners realized that despite their victory, the greater battles that would inevitably come would mean greater losses for their side as well.

Beauregard was considered the hero of the battle and was promoted that day by President Davis to full general in the Confederate Army. Stonewall Jackson, arguably the most important tactical contributor to the victory, received no special recognition, but would later achieve glory for his 1862 Valley Campaign. Irvin McDowell bore the brunt of the blame for the Union defeat and was soon replaced by Maj. Gen. George B. McClellan, who was named general-in-chief of all the Union armies. McDowell was also present to bear significant blame for the defeat of Maj. Gen. John Pope's Army of Virginia by Gen. Robert E. Lee's Army of Northern Virginia thirteen months later, at the Second Battle of Bull Run. Patterson was also removed from command

The name of the battle has caused controversy since 1861. The Union Army frequently named battles after significant rivers and creeks that played a role in the fighting; the Confederates generally used the names of nearby towns or farms. The U.S. National Park Service uses the Confederate name for its national battlefield park, but the Union name (Bull Run) also has widespread name in popular literature.

Battlefield confusion between the battle flags, especially the similarity of the Confederacy's "Stars and Bars" and the Union's "Stars and Stripes" when fluttering, led to the adoption of the Confederate Battle Flag, which eventually became the most popular symbol of the Confederacy and the South in general.

"What If"?

Now this is historically what happened.

<u>What if</u> the Confederates, under the leadership of President Jefferson Davis and the Officers decided to do something completely unexpected on the so called Black Monday?

What if the Southern Army made a power play and marched on Washington while their army (Union) was in shambles.

Here is what could have happened. The routed Union Army was still licking its wounds. No one expected to see the Rebel Army coming in sight of the U.S. Capital.

Let's say, The Southern Army was all together and marching in strength on Monday and the Union pickets sounded the alarm long before the Confederates were in shooting range.

The Union Army became so alarmed that another route was started and they ran through Washington City like rats on a sinking ship.

President Lincoln tried to get General McDowell and his officers to take control of the migrating Union Army, but to no avail.

The Army was like a mob stampeding for their lives.

The House of Representatives, the Senate, the Judges and all the United States Government began to flee Washington City.

As before, the civilian carriages and wagons were contributing to the panic.

What could President Lincoln do?

The United States Army got a small 1000 man, but brave, army together, set up a few cannon and Mister Lincoln came out to give commands. This Army would protect the President at all cost. Here they stood facing thousands of gray clad soldiers.

"The Union was in a tight spot!"

**President Jefferson Davis President of
the Confederate States of America**

President Abraham Lincoln

President of the United States

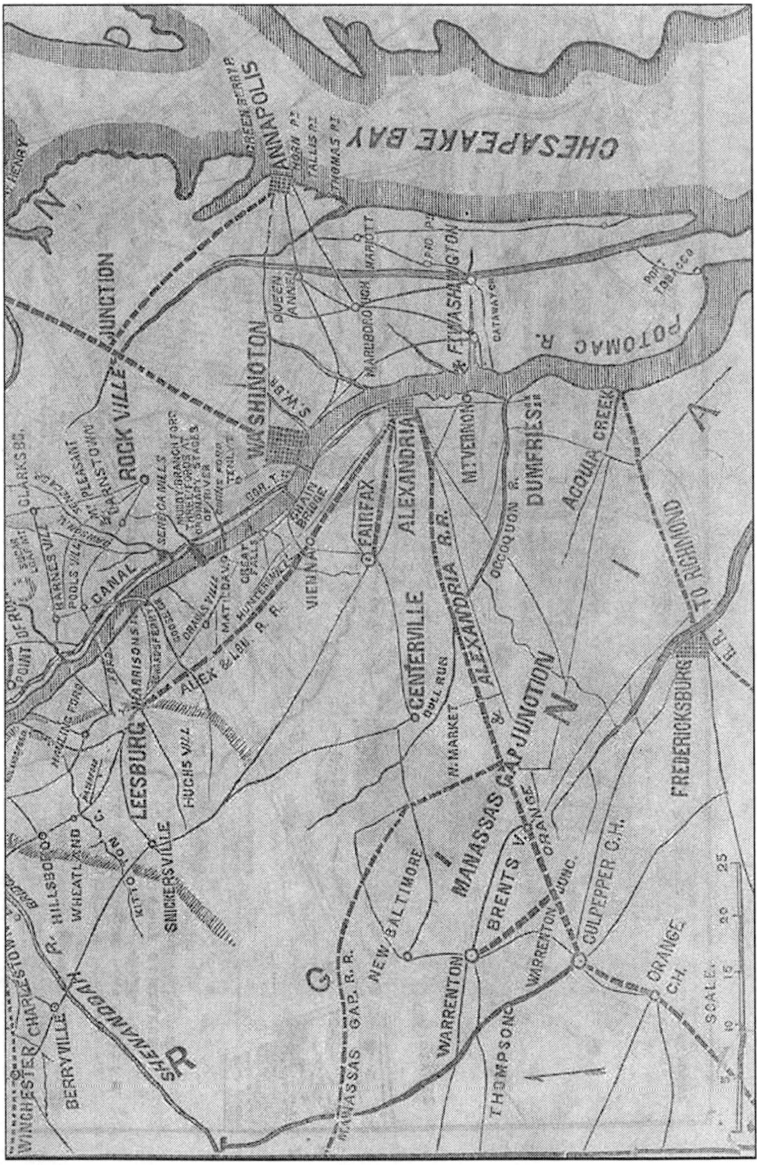
CHESAPEAKE BAY
ANNAPOLIS
POTOMAC R.
WASHINGTON
ROCK VILLE
JUNCTION
ALEXANDRIA
FAIRFAX
CENTERVILLE
MT VERNON
DUMFRIES
ACQUIA CREEK
TO RICHMOND
FREDERICKSBURG
ALEXANDRIA R.R.
& ALEXANDRIA
MANASSAS GAP JUNCTION
BRENTS V.
CULPEPPER C.H.
ORANGE C.H.
WARRENTON
WARRENTON JUNC.
NEW BALTIMORE
THOMPSONS
MANASSAS GAP R.R.
LEESBURG
SNICKERSVILLE
WHEATLAND
HILLSBORO
BERRYVILLE
WINCHESTER
CHARLESTOWN
SHENANDOAH
CANAL
VIENNA
DRAINSVILLE
ALEX & LOU. R.R.
POINT OF ROCKS
SCALE.

General Winfield Scott

On November 1, 1861, President Abraham
Lincoln ordered the retirement of Lieutenant
General Scott by Major General George B.
McClellan. Scott's health had been steadily
failing and he was no longer up to campaigning
in the field. He was also being undermined by his
youthful subordinate McClellan, who clearly
coveted his superior's post.

"What If"?

Where was General Robert E. Lee, while all of this was going on? He was a Staff Officer and personal adviser to President Jefferson Davis. He was working on long term plans if they were needed.

First National Flag of the Confederate States of America.

Colors were Red and white Bars, Blue back ground with white stars.

"What If"?

Confederate General Joseph E. Johnston

From Wikipedia, the free encyclopedia

Pierre Gustave Toutant Beauregard   May 28, 1818 – February 20, 1893) was a Louisiana-born American military officer, politician, inventor, writer, civil servant, and the first prominent general of the Confederate States Army .

"What If"?

The Confederate Army drew close with Calvary leading the march. There was a young Confederate Calvary Colonel by the name of J.E.B. Stuart along with General's Beauregard, and Johnston, leading at least 25,000 soldiers.

President Lincoln and his small contingent of officers and men were standing strong, but knew they could not stand-off such an army that confronted them.

Tension ran high in the line defending Washington City. Still the powerful Southern Army continued to close in on the little blue army and Mister Lincoln.

When the Confederate Army came within the range of cannon the command was given to halt. The generals out in front talked and gave a letter to Colonel J.E.B. Stuart and up came a white flag of truce. The gallant Colonel Stuart had been instrumental in causing the hasty retreat yesterday by the Union Army. His Calvary had charged fearlessly into the flank of the Union Army.

Now Colonel Stuart along with ten of his men rode toward the waiting Union Army. One of Stuart's men rode beside him holding the white flag high.

While Colonel Stuart and his men make their way at a trot toward the line, I must interject something else of mighty importance. There was one other Colonel on the field yesterday that must take a lot of credit for sending the Blue uniformed men skedaddling.

Colonel Thomas Jonathon Jackson rose to prominence and earned his most famous nickname at the Battle of Manassas on July 21, 1861. As the Confederate lines began to crumble under heavy Union assault, Jackson's brigade provided crucial reinforcements on Henry House Hill, demonstrating the discipline he instilled in his men. Brig. Gen. Barnard Elliott Bee, Jr., exhorted his own troops to re-form by shouting, *"There is Jackson standing like a stone wall. Let us determine to die here, and we will conquer. Rally behind the Virginians."*

Colonel J.E.B. Stuart has reached the line of soldiers and is greeted by Union Colonel William T. Sherman.

Colonel Stuart speaks, "Hello Sir, I am Colonel Stuart with a letter for your President Lincoln. It is for him only, I request to ride alone through your line and be escorted to him."

"What If"?

Colonel, Thomas Jonathan "Stonewall Jackson"

Union General McDowell

"Well Sir, I will take the letter to him, I will not let you cross over," said the Colonel William T. Sherman.

"I have been instructed by my command and even my President Jefferson Davis to put the letter in Mister Lincoln's hand," Said a determined Colonel Stuart with his eyes shooting daggers at the Union Colonel.

"Well Colonel Stuart, you dismount and give me your weapons, I will try to get you to President Lincoln," said the nervous Union Colonel.

J.E.B. Stuart dismounted and handed his sword and two pistols to one of his men and approached the Colonel. The Colonel looked him over and yielded him passage through the thin line.

 The Union Colonel said, "Wait here Sir, and grabbed a young private and told him to run back and see if Mister Lincoln would invite Colonel Stuart to a meeting behind the line.

The private was off like a flash and in about five minutes he was back.
"Colonel Sir, President Lincoln will see Colonel Stuart, but you and four soldiers are to escort him back," said the young private.

Colonel J.E.B. Stuart

"What If"?

The Colonel told the private and three other soldiers that were handy to go with him and escort the Rebel Colonel to the president.

Union Colonel Sherman walked in front of Colonel Stuart and he had two soldiers on each side as they walked.

Colonel Stuart walked proudly as the wind blew his heavy beard and his plume in his fancy hat.

President Lincoln was standing tall and seemed to show no fear as the escort party and Colonel Stuart approached.

In the background were plenty of armed soldiers and also Vice-President Johnson, General McDowell, and General Winfield Scott were there.

Colonel J.E.B. Stuart came to attention and gave Mister Lincoln a hardy salute and Lincoln tipped his brim on the tall stove pipe hat.

"What do you have for me, Sir?" asked an anxious President Lincoln?

"I have a letter for your hands only, Sir," answered Colonel Stuart.

J.E.B. Stuart handed the lanky, Abraham Lincoln the letter and took two steps back to await an answer from Mister Lincoln.

Looking on was Vice-president Johnson (A Southerner), and General Winfield Scott.

Abraham Lincoln took the letter, pulled out his spec tickles and put them on his weary face one wire piece at a time and opened the letter carefully and scanned it one word at a time.

Colonel Stuart felt that the little Army around Lincoln knew that they were in a tight spot.

As they looked back to the south they could see that the Confederate Army had moved much artillery to the fore front.

After handing the letter to Mister Johnson and he handed it to the General, Winfield Scott, they both read it and made facial expressions of gloom. Lincoln told Colonel Stuart that he would meet with President Jefferson Davis.

The terms the Confederate States required from the United States were spelled out; only little details would have to be worked out. The Confederate States of America was speaking from Strength, after Stampeding the Northern Army all the way to the far end of Washington City. What were the terms spelled out in the letter composed by President Jefferson Davis?

1. The Confederate States of America do not require the United States to surrender, but to yield all the states the right to secede and be recognized as an Independent Nation.
2. The Confederate States of America require that all hostilities cease and that all Union troops and ships be removed from Confederate territory at once.
3. The United States will allow any State or territory to join the Confederate States of America in the future and trade between the nations will commence as soon as possible.
4. A meeting of Heads of State shall meet and work out any and all details.
5. If this is agreeable with the United States, The President must sign and at least ten other Officers must also sign as witness, this action must be done this very Day, July 22, 1861; or The Confederate Army will march at once and attack Washington City with any and all force they have.

Signed: *Jefferson Davis, President, Confederate States of America.*

Colonel J.E.B. Stuart spoke up, "Mister President Sir, I was instructed to have you and the witness's sign and then meet half way between our forces. President Jefferson Davis and ten Officers will meet you and ten officers for the Decoration Ceremony, Sir."

"Sir, if you will look out at about half way between Your force and our's you will see a table set up with our President waiting for you and your party, Sir," said Colonel Stuart.

"Pretty Damn sure of himself ain't he?" said Abraham Lincoln.

Colonel Stuart gave him a smile and said, "Sir, I think the odds are against you and there need not be any more bloodshed."

Abraham Lincoln and ten officials and officers signed the document. Horses and a carriage were brought to the front for President Lincoln and his party to ride to the meeting table.

Mister Lincoln, Vice-President Johnson, General Winfield Scott, and General McDowell all loaded into the Carriage and ten other officials and officers rode their horses, all following J.E.B. Stuart to meet the

"What If"?

President and Officials of the new nation called the Confederate States of America.

**Vice President
Andrew Johnson**

The Vice-President of the United States was Southern Born. He won the election on his own as they did not run together as they do today.

He would work to make things right between the two countries.

"The South Won"

Two flags and two nations met that day between the lines of a small Union Army and a large Confederate Army to make peace and set out on a new journey of history.

The two leaders of two nations set down at a small wobbling table and signed two copies and both sides had ten officials or officers sign the Official Papers as witness.

It is Official; The Confederate States of America is a Nation now.

The two Presidents shook hands and as they parted, President Lincoln said, "Sir, I pray you all know what you are doing, good luck."

Jefferson Davis smiled at the saddened Lincoln and said, "Sir, we do know what we are doing and we have gained our God given freedoms, Good luck to you Sir."

A date and place had been set up for the officials of both nations to get together and start working out details.

The two groups divided and the Confederates rode back to their awaiting army. The jubilant shouts from the happy Confederates sounded almost like thunder.

Abraham Lincoln and the Federals all turned when they heard the awesome sounds of the southern shouts. They could see Confederate flags waving high above the army.

Telegraphs were sent all over the South and North. The War is over and two nations share North America.

In the south, church bells begin to toll and folks beat on pots and pans to make their joyful noises.

There would be prayer meetings all of the South and the North. The South would be thanking and praising God; The North would be praying for hope and guidance.

States that had teetered on the decision of which side to join now came forward. West Virginia, Maryland, Missouri, and Kentucky would now join the Confederate States of America.

Some of the western territories that would form States will go with the United States and some would go with the Confederate States of America.

The new Capitol of the United States will be moved back to New York City and the

Confederate Capitol will remain in
RIchmond, Virginia.

The News would be in broad lettered
headlines in every paper in America and
around the world.

That was one, "What If!"

The South wins the war at Gettysburg!

Battle of Gettysburg

The **Battle of Gettysburg** was fought July 1–3, 1863, in and around the town of Gettysburg, Pennsylvania. The battle with the largest number of casualties in the American Civil War, it is often described as the war's turning point. Union Maj. Gen. George Gordon Meade's Army of the Potomac defeated attacks by Confederate Gen. Robert E. Lee's Army of Northern Virginia, ending Lee's invasion of the North.

After his success at Chancellorsville in Virginia in May 1863, Lee led his army through the Shenandoah Valley to begin his second invasion of the North; the Gettysburg Campaign.

With his army in high spirits, Lee intended to shift the focus of the summer campaign from war-ravaged northern Virginia and hoped to influence Northern politicians to give up their prosecution of the war by penetrating as far as Harrisburg, Pennsylvania, or even Philadelphia.

Prodded by President Abraham Lincoln, Maj. Gen. Joseph Hooker moved his army in pursuit, but was relieved just three days before the battle and replaced by General Meade.

Elements of the two armies initially collided at Gettysburg on July 1, 1863, as Lee urgently concentrated his forces there, his objective being to engage the Union army and destroy it. Low ridges to the northwest of town were defended initially by a Union cavalry division under Brig. Gen. John Buford, and soon reinforced with two corps of Union infantry. However, two large Confederate corps assaulted them from the northwest and north, collapsing the hastily developed Union lines, sending the defenders retreating through the streets of town to the hills just to the south.

On the second day of battle, most of both armies had assembled. The Union line was laid out in a defensive formation resembling a fishhook. In the late afternoon of July 2, Lee launched a heavy assault on the Union left flank, and fierce fighting raged at Little Round Top, the Wheatfield, Devil's Den, and the Peach Orchard. On the Union right, demonstrations escalated into full scale assaults on Culp's Hill and Cemetery Hill. All

"What If"?

across the battlefield, despite significant losses, the Union defenders held their lines.

On the third day of battle, July 3, fighting resumed on Culp's Hill, and cavalry battles raged to the east and south, but the main event was a dramatic infantry assault by 12,500 Confederates against the center of the Union line on Cemetery Ridge, known as Pickett's Charge. The charge was repulsed by Union rifle and artillery fire, at great losses to the Confederate army. Lee led his army on a torturous retreat back to Virginia. Between 46,000 and 51,000 soldiers from both armies were casualties in the three day battle. That November, President Lincoln used the dedication ceremony for the Gettysburg National Cemetery to honor the fallen Union soldiers and redefine the purpose of the war in his historic Gettysburg Address.

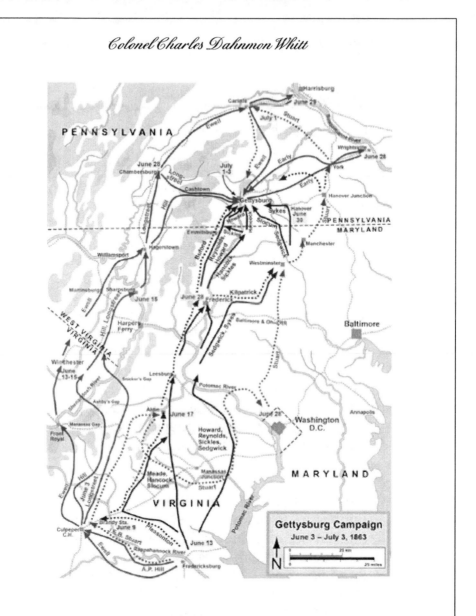

Gettysburg Campaign (through July 3);
cavalry movements shown with dashed
lines.

Shortly after the Army of Northern Virginia won a major victory over the Army of the Potomac at the Battle of Chancellorsville (April 30 – May 6, 1863), Robert E. Lee decided upon a second invasion of the North (the first was the unsuccessful Maryland Campaign of September 1862, which ended in the bloody Battle of Antietam). Such a move would upset Federal plans for the summer campaigning season and possibly reduce the pressure on the besieged Confederate garrison at Vicksburg. The invasion would allow the Confederates to live off the bounty of the rich Northern farms while giving war-ravaged Virginia a much-needed rest. In addition, Lee's 72,000-man army could threaten Philadelphia, Baltimore, and Washington, and <u>possibly strengthen the growing peace movement in the North.</u> (Protesters were in all the large cities)

On June 3, Lee's army began to shift northward from Fredericksburg, Virginia. To attain more efficiency in his command, Lee had reorganized his two large corps into three new corps. Lt. Gen. James Longstreet retained command of his First Corps. The old corps of deceased Thomas J. "Stonewall" Jackson was divided in two, with the Second Corps going to Lt. Gen. Richard S. Ewell and the new Third Corps to Lt. Gen.

A.P. Hill. The Cavalry Division was commanded by Maj. Gen. J.E.B. Stuart.

The Union Army of the Potomac, under Maj. Gen. Joseph Hooker, consisted of seven infantry corps, a cavalry corps, and an Artillery Reserve, for a combined strength of about 94,000 men; However, President Lincoln replaced Hooker with Maj. Gen. George Gordon Meade, a Pennsylvanian, because of Hooker's defeat at Chancellorsville and his timid response to Lee's second invasion north of the Potomac River.

The first major action of the campaign took place on June 9 between cavalry forces at Brandy Station, near Culpeper, Virginia. The 9,500 Confederate cavalrymen under Stuart were surprised by Maj. Gen. Alfred Pleasonton's combined arms force of two cavalry divisions (8,000 troopers) and 3,000 infantry, but Stuart eventually repulsed the Union attack. The inconclusive battle, the largest predominantly cavalry engagement of the war, proved for the first time that the Union horse soldier was equal to his Southern counterpart.

By mid-June, the Army of Northern Virginia was poised to cross the Potomac River and enter Maryland. After defeating the Federal garrisons at Winchester and Martinsburg, Ewell's Second Corps began crossing the river on June 15. Hill's and Longstreet's corps followed on June 24 and June 25. Hooker's army pursued, keeping between the U.S. capital and Lee's army. The Federals crossed the Potomac from June 25 to June 27.

Lee gave strict orders for his army to minimize any negative impacts on the civilian population. Food, horses, and other supplies were generally not seized outright, although quartermasters reimbursing Northern farmers and merchants with Confederate money were not well received. Various towns, most notably York, Pennsylvania, were required to pay indemnities in lieu of supplies, under threat of destruction. During the invasion, the Confederates seized some 40 northern African Americans, a few of whom were escaped fugitive slaves but most were freemen. They were sent south into slavery under guard.

On June 26, elements of Maj. Gen. Jubal Early's division of Ewell's Corps occupied the town of Gettysburg after chasing off newly raised Pennsylvania militia in a series of minor skirmishes. Early laid the borough under tribute but did not collect any significant supplies. Soldiers burned several railroad cars and a covered bridge, and destroyed nearby rails and telegraph lines. The following morning, Jubal Early departed for adjacent York County.

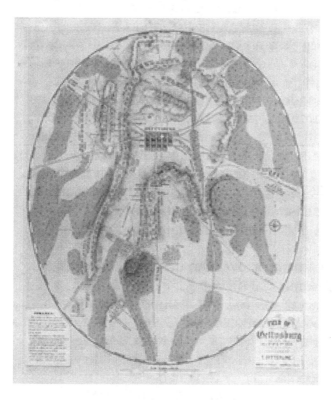

This 1863 oval-shaped map depicts Gettysburg Battlefield during July 1–3, 1863, showing troop and artillery positions and movements, drainage, roads, railroads, and houses with the names of residents at the time of the Battle of Gettysburg.

"What If"?

Meanwhile, in a controversial move, Lee allowed Jeb Stuart to take a portion of the army's cavalry and ride around the east flank of the Union army. Lee's orders gave Stuart much latitude, and both generals share the blame for the long absence of Stuart's cavalry, as well as for the failure to assign a more active role to the cavalry left with the army. Stuart and his three best brigades were absent from the army during the crucial phase of the approach to Gettysburg and the first two days of battle. By June 29, Lee's army was strung out in an arc from Chambersburg (28 miles northwest of Gettysburg) to Carlisle (30 miles north of Gettysburg) to near Harrisburg and Wrightsville on the Susquehanna River.

In a dispute over the use of the forces defending the Harpers Ferry garrison, Hooker offered his resignation, and Abraham Lincoln and General-in-Chief Henry W. Halleck, who were looking for an excuse to get rid of him, immediately accepted. They replaced Hooker early on the morning of June 28 with Maj. Gen. George Gordon Meade, then commander of the V Corps.

On June 29, when Lee learned that the Army of the Potomac had crossed the Potomac River, he ordered a concentration of his forces around Cashtown, located at the eastern base of South Mountain and eight miles west of Gettysburg. On June 30, while part of Hill's Corps was in Cashtown, one of Hill's brigades, North Carolinians under Brig. Gen. J. Johnston Pettigrew, ventured toward Gettysburg. In his memoirs, Maj. Gen. Henry Heth, Pettigrew's division commander, claimed that he sent Pettigrew to search for supplies in town; especially shoes.

When Pettigrew's troops approached Gettysburg on June 30, they noticed Union cavalry under Brig. Gen. John Buford arriving south of town, and Pettigrew returned to Cashtown without engaging them. When Pettigrew told Hill and Heth what he had seen, neither general believed that there was a substantial Federal force in or near the town, suspecting that it had been only Pennsylvania militia. Despite General Lee's order to avoid a general engagement until his entire army was concentrated, Hill decided to mount a significant reconnaissance in force the following morning to determine the size and strength of the enemy force in his front. Around 5 a.m. on Wednesday, July 1, two brigades of Heth's division advanced to Gettysburg.

First day of battle

"What If"?

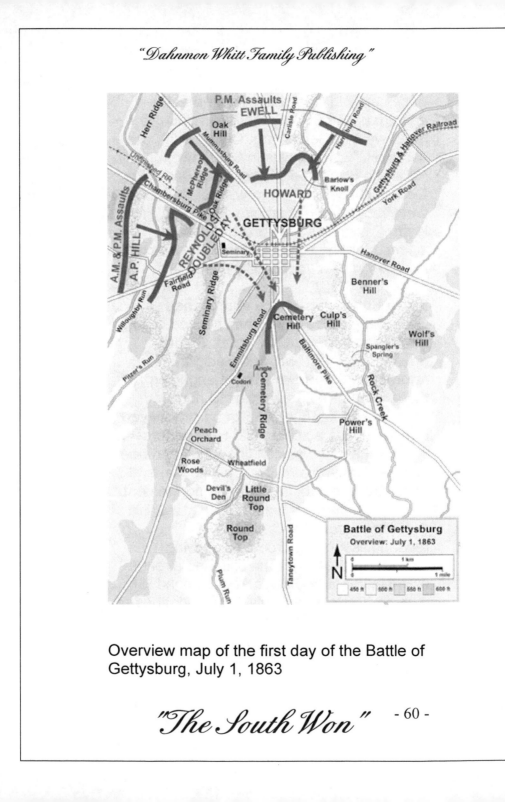

Overview map of the first day of the Battle of Gettysburg, July 1, 1863

"The South Won" - 60 -

Anticipating that the Confederates would march on Gettysburg from the west on the morning of July 1, Buford laid out his defenses on three ridges west of the town: Herr Ridge, McPherson Ridge, and Seminary Ridge. These were appropriate terrain for a delaying action by his small cavalry division against superior Confederate infantry forces, meant to buy time awaiting the arrival of Union infantrymen who could occupy the strong defensive positions south of town at Cemetery Hill, Cemetery Ridge, and Culp's Hill. Buford understood that if the Confederates could gain control of these heights, Meade's army would have difficulty dislodging them.

Heth's division advanced with two brigades forward, commanded by Brig. Generals James J. Archer and Joseph R. Davis. They preceded easterly in columns along the Chambersburg Pike. Three miles west of town, about 7:30 a.m. on July 1, the two brigades met light resistance from Union cavalry, and deployed into line. According to lore, the Union soldier to fire the first shot of the battle was Lt. Marcellus Jones. In 1886 Lt. Jones returned to Gettysburg to mark the spot where he fired the first shot with a monument. Eventually, Heth's men reached dismounted troopers of Col. William Gamble's cavalry brigade, who raised determined resistance and delaying tactics from behind fence posts with fire from their breechloading carbines. Still, by 10:20 a.m., the Confederates had pushed the Union cavalrymen east to McPherson Ridge, when the vanguard of the I Corps (Maj. Gen. John F. Reynolds) finally arrived

North of the pike, Davis gained a temporary success against Brig. Gen. Lysander Cutler's brigade but was repulsed with heavy losses in an action around an unfinished railroad bed cut in the ridge. South of the pike, Archer's brigade assaulted through Herbst (also known as McPherson's) Woods. The Federal Iron Brigade under Brig. Gen. Solomon Meredith enjoyed initial success against Archer, capturing several hundred men, including Archer himself

General Reynolds was shot and killed early in the fighting while directing troop and artillery placements just to the east of the woods. Shelby Foote wrote that the Union cause lost a man considered by many to be *"the best general in the army."* Maj. Gen. Abner Doubleday assumed command. Fighting in the Chambersburg Pike area lasted until about 12:30 p.m. It resumed around 2:30 p.m., when Heth's entire division engaged, adding the brigades of Pettigrew and Col. John M. Brockenbrough.

As Pettigrew's North Carolina Brigade came on line, they flanked the 19th Indiana and drove the Iron Brigade back. The 26th North Carolina (the largest regiment in the army with 839 men) lost heavily, leaving the first day's fight with around 212 men. By the end of the three-day battle, they had about 152 men standing, the highest casualty percentage for one battle of any regiment, North or South.

Slowly the Iron Brigade was pushed out of the woods toward Seminary Ridge. Hill added Maj. Gen. William Dorsey Pender's division to the assault, and the I Corps was

"What If"?

driven back through the grounds of the Lutheran Seminary and Gettysburg streets.

As the fighting to the west proceeded, two divisions of Ewell's Second Corps, marching west toward Cashtown in accordance with Lee's order for the army to concentrate in that vicinity, turned south on the Carlisle and Harrisburg roads toward Gettysburg, while the Union XI Corps (Maj. Gen. Oliver O. Howard) raced north on the Baltimore Pike and Taneytown Road.

By early afternoon, the Federal line ran in a semicircle west, north, and northeast of Gettysburg.

However, the Federals did not have enough troops; Cutler, who was deployed north of the Chambersburg Pike. The far left division of the XI Corps was unable to deploy in time to strengthen the line, so Doubleday was forced to throw in reserve brigades to salvage his line.

Around 2 p.m., the Confederate Second Corps divisions of Maj. Gens. Robert E. Rodes and Jubal Early assaulted and out-flanked the Union I and XI Corps positions north and northwest of town. The Confederate brigades of Col. Edward A. O'Neal and Brig. Gen. Alfred Iverson suffered severe losses assaulting the I Corps division of Brig. Gen. John C. Robinson south of Oak Hill. Early's division profited from a blunder by Brig. Gen. Francis C. Barlow, when he advanced his XI Corps division to Blocher's Knoll (directly north of town and now known as Barlow's Knoll); this represented a salient in the corps line, susceptible to attack from multiple sides, and Early's troops overran Barlow's division, which constituted the right flank of the Union Army's position. Barlow was wounded and captured in the attack.

As Federal positions collapsed both north and west of town, Gen. Howard ordered a retreat to the high ground south of town at Cemetery Hill, where he had left the division of Brig. Gen. Adolph von Steinwehr in reserve. Maj. Gen. Winfield S. Hancock assumed command of the battlefield, sent by Meade when he heard that Reynolds had been killed. Hancock, commander of the II Corps and Meade's most trusted subordinate, was ordered to take command of the field and to determine whether Gettysburg was an appropriate place for a major battle. Hancock told Howard, "I think this the strongest position by nature upon which to fight a battle that I ever saw." When Howard agreed, Hancock concluded the discussion: *"Very well, sir, I select this as the*

"What If"?

battle-field." Hancock's determination had a morale-boosting effect on the retreating Union soldiers, but he played no direct tactical role on the first day.

General Lee understood the defensive potential to the Union if they held this high ground. He sent orders to Ewell that Cemetery Hill be taken *"if practicable."* Ewell, who had previously served under Stonewall Jackson, a general well known for issuing peremptory orders, determined such an assault was not practicable and, thus, did not attempt it; this decision is considered by historians to be a great missed opportunity.

The first day at Gettysburg, more significant than simply a prelude to the bloody second and third days, ranks as the 23rd biggest battle of the war by number of troops engaged. About one quarter of Meade's army (22,000 men) and one third of Lee's army (27,000) were engaged

Second day of battle

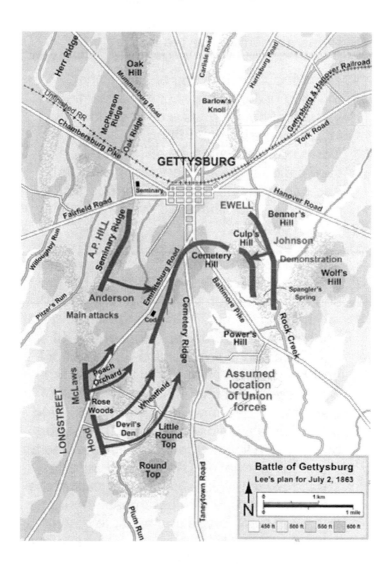

Robert E. Lee's plan for July 2, 1863

"What If"?

Plans and movement to battle

Throughout the evening of July 1 and morning of July 2, most of the remaining infantry of both armies arrived on the field, including the Union II, III, V, VI, and XII Corps. Longstreet's third division, commanded by Maj. Gen. George Pickett, had begun the march from Chambersburg early in the morning; it did not arrive until late on July 2.

The Union line ran from Culp's Hill southeast of the town, northwest to Cemetery Hill just south of town, then south for nearly two miles along Cemetery Ridge, terminating just north of Little Round Top. Most of the XII Corps was on Culp's Hill; the remnants of I and XI Corps defended Cemetery Hill; II Corps covered most of the northern half of Cemetery Ridge; and III Corps was ordered to take up a position to its flank. The shape of the Union line is popularly described as a "fishhook" formation. The Confederate line paralleled the Union line about a mile to the west on Seminary Ridge, ran east through the town, then curved southeast to a point opposite Culp's Hill. Thus, the Federal army had interior lines, while the Confederate line was nearly five miles long.

Lee's battle plan for July 2 called for Longstreet's First Corps to position itself stealthily to attack the Union left flank, facing northeast straddling the Emmitsburg Road, and to roll up the Federal line. The attack sequence was to begin with Major General's John Bell Hood's and Lafayette McLaws's divisions, followed by Major General Richard H. Anderson's division of Hill's Third Corps. The progressive sequence of this attack would prevent Meade from shifting troops from his center to bolster his left. At the same time, Major General Edward "Allegheny" Johnson's and Jubal Early's Second Corps divisions were to make a demonstration against Culp's and Cemetery Hills (again, to prevent the shifting of Federal troops), and to turn the demonstration into a full-scale attack if a favorable opportunity presented itself.

Lee's plan, however, was based on faulty intelligence, because of General Stuart's continued absence from the battlefield. Instead of moving beyond the Federals' left and attacking their flank, Longstreet's left division, under McLaws, would face Major Genoral Daniel Sickles's III Corps directly in their path. Sickles had been dissatisfied with the position assigned to him on the southern end of Cemetery Ridge. Seeing higher ground more favorable to artillery positions a

"What If"?

half mile to the west, he advanced his corps(without orders) to the slightly higher ground along the Emmitsburg Road. The new line ran from Devil's Den, northwest to the Sherfy farm's Peach Orchard, then northeast along the Emmitsburg Road to south of the Codori farm. This created an untenable front at the Peach Orchard; Brig. Gen. Andrew A. Humphreys's division (in position along the Emmitsburg Road) and Major General David B. Birney's division (to the south) were subject to attacks from two sides and were spread out over a longer front than their small corps could defend effectively.

Longstreet's attack was to be made as early as practicable; however, Longstreet got permission from Lee to await the arrival of one of his brigades, and while marching to the assigned position, his men came within sight of a Union signal station on Little Round Top. Countermarching to avoid detection wasted much time, and Hood's and McLaws's divisions did not launch their attacks until just after 4 p.m. and 5 p.m., respectively.

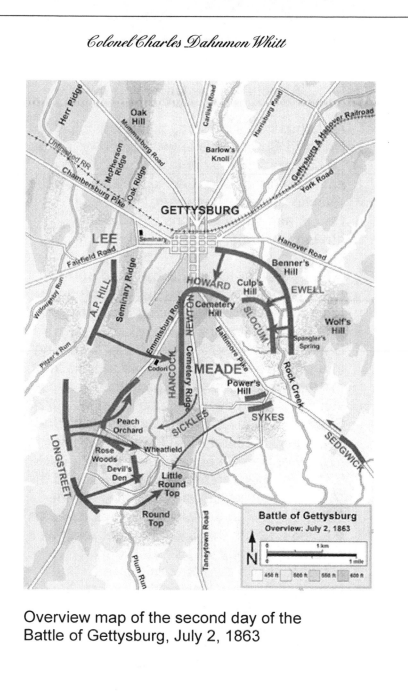

Overview map of the second day of the
Battle of Gettysburg, July 2, 1863

"What If"?

Attacks on the Union left flank

As Longstreet's divisions slammed into the Union III Corps, Meade was forced to send 20,000 reinforcements in the form of the entire V Corps, Brig. Gen. John C. Caldwell's division of the II Corps, most of the XII Corps, and small portions of the newly arrived VI Corps.

The Confederate assault deviated from Lee's plan since Hood's division moved more easterly than intended, losing its alignment with the Emmitsburg Road, attacking Devil's Den and Little Round Top. McLaws, coming in on Hood's left, drove multiple attacks into the thinly stretched III Corps in the Wheatfield and overwhelmed them in Sherfy's Peach Orchard. McLaws's attack eventually reached Plum Run Valley (the "Valley of Death") before being beaten back by the Pennsylvania Reserves division of the V Corps, moving down from Little Round Top. The III Corps was virtually destroyed as a combat unit in this battle. Sickles's leg was amputated after it was shattered by a cannonball. Caldwell's division was destroyed in the Wheatfield. Anderson's division, coming from McLaws's left and starting forward around 6 p.m., reached the crest of Cemetery Ridge, but it could not hold the position in the face of counterattacks from the II Corps, including an almost suicidal bayonet charge by the small 1st Minnesota regiment against a Confederate brigade, ordered in desperation by Hancock to buy time for reinforcements to arrive.

As fighting raged in the Wheatfield and Devil's Den, Colonel Strong Vincent of V Corps had a precarious hold on Little Round Top, an important hill at the extreme left of the Union line. His brigade of four relatively small regiments was able to resist repeated assaults by Brig. Gen. Evander M. Law's brigade of Hood's division.

Meade's chief engineer, Brig. Gen. G. K. Warren, had realized the importance of this position, and dispatched Vincent's brigade, an artillery battery, and the 140th New York to occupy Little Round Top mere minutes before Hood's troops arrived. The defense of Little Round Top with a bayonet charge by the 20th Maine was one of the most fabled episodes in the Civil War and propelled Colonel Joshua L. Chamberlain into prominence after the war.

"What If"?

Attacks on the Union right flank

Union breastworks on Culp's Hill

About 7:00 p.m., the Second Corps' attack by Johnson's division on Culp's Hill got off to a late start. Most of the hill's defenders, the Union XII Corps, had been sent to the left to defend against Longstreet's attacks, and the only portion of the corps remaining on the hill was a brigade of New Yorkers under Brig. Gen. George S. Greene. Because of Greene's insistence on constructing strong defensive works, and with reinforcements from the I and XI Corps, Greene's men held off the Confederate attackers, although the

Southerners did capture a portion of the abandoned Federal works on the lower part of Culp's Hill.

Just at dark, two of Jubal Early's brigades attacked the Union XI Corps positions on East Cemetery Hill where Col. Andrew L. Harris of the 2nd Brigade, 1st Division, came under a withering attack, losing half his men; however, Early failed to support his brigades in their attack, and Ewell's remaining division, that of Maj. Gen. Robert E. Rodes, failed to aid Early's attack by moving against Cemetery Hill from the west. The Union army's interior lines enabled its commanders to shift troops quickly to critical areas, and with reinforcements from II Corps, the Federal troops retained possession of East Cemetery Hill, and Early's brigades were forced to withdraw.

<u>Jeb Stuart and his three cavalry brigades arrived in Gettysburg around noon but had no role in the second day's battle.</u> Brig. Gen. Wade Hampton's brigade fought a minor engagement with newly promoted 23-year-old Brig. Gen. George Armstrong Custer's Michigan cavalry near Hunterstown to the northeast of Gettysburg.

"What If"?

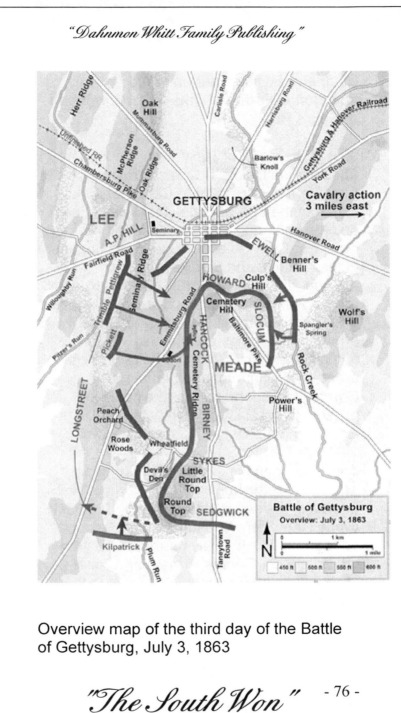

Overview map of the third day of the Battle
of Gettysburg, July 3, 1863

Third day of battle as it happened

General Lee wished to renew the attack on Friday, July 3, using the same basic plan as the previous day: General Longstreet would attack the Federal left, while Ewell attacked Culp's Hill. However, before Longstreet was ready, Union XII Corps troops started a dawn artillery bombardment against the Confederates on Culp's Hill in an effort to regain a portion of their lost works. The Confederates attacked, and the second fight for Culp's Hill ended around 11 a.m., after some seven hours of bitter combat.

Lee was forced to change his plans. <u>Under protest, Longstreet would command Pickett's Virginia division</u> of his own First Corps, plus six brigades from Hill's Corps, in an attack on the Federal II Corps position at the right center of the Union line on Cemetery Ridge. Prior to the attack, all the artillery the Confederacy could bring to bear on the Federal positions would bombard and weaken the enemy's line.

"What If"?

The "High Water Mark" on Cemetery Ridge as it appears today. The monument to the 72nd Pennsylvania Volunteer Infantry Regiment ("Baxter's Philadelphia Fire Zouaves") appears at right, the Copse of Trees to the left.

Around 1 p.m., from 150 to 170 Confederate guns began an artillery bombardment that was probably the largest of the war. (The thunderous noise could be heard 100 miles away)

In order to save valuable ammunition for the infantry attack that they knew would follow, the Army of the Potomac's artillery, under the command of Brig. Gen. Henry Jackson Hunt, at first did not return the enemy's fire. After waiting about 15 minutes, about 80

Federal cannons added to the Thunder. The Army of Northern Virginia was critically low on artillery ammunition, and the cannonade did not significantly affect the Union position. (Timers on the shells were off and exploded behind the Federals.)

Around 3 p.m., the cannon fire subsided, and 12,500 Southern soldiers stepped from the ridgeline and advanced the three-quarters of a mile to Cemetery Ridge in what is known to history as "Pickett's Charge". (They marched as if on parade.)

As the Confederates approached, there was fierce flanking artillery fire from Union positions on Cemetery Hill and north of Little Round Top, and musket and canister fire from Hancock's II Corps. In the Union center, the commander of artillery had held fire during the Confederate bombardment, leading Southern commanders to believe the Northern cannon batteries had been knocked out. However, they opened fire on the Confederate infantry during their approach with devastating results. Nearly one half of the attackers did not return to their own lines. Although the Federal line wavered and broke temporarily at a jog called the "Angle" in a low stone fence, just north of a patch of vegetation called the Copse of Trees, reinforcements rushed into

"What If"?

the breach, and the Confederate attack was repulsed. The farthest advance of Brig. Gen. Lewis A. Armistead's brigade of Maj. Gen. George Pickett's division at the Angle is referred to as the "High-water mark of the Confederacy", arguably representing the closest the South ever came to its goal of achieving independence from the Union via military victory.

There were two significant cavalry engagements on July 3. Stuart was sent to guard the Confederate left flank and was to be prepared to exploit any success the infantry might achieve on Cemetery Hill by flanking the Federal right and hitting their trains and lines of communications. Three miles east of Gettysburg, in what is now called "East Cavalry Field" (not shown on the accompanying map, but between the York and Hanover Roads), Stuart's forces collided with Federal cavalry: Brig. Gen. David McMurtrie Gregg's division and Brig. Gen. Custer's brigade. A lengthy mounted battle, including hand-to-hand sabre combat, ensued. Custer's charge, leading the 1st Michigan Cavalry, blunted the attack by Wade Hampton's brigade, blocking Stuart from achieving his objectives in the Federal rear. Meanwhile, after hearing news of the day's victory, Brig. Gen. Judson Kilpatrick launched a cavalry attack against the infantry positions of Longstreet's Corps southwest of Big Round Top. Brig. Gen. Elon J. Farnsworth protested against the futility of such a move but obeyed orders. Farnsworth was killed in the attack, and his brigade suffered significant losses.

Aftermath Casualties

"The Harvest of Death": Union dead on the battlefield at Gettysburg, Pennsylvania, photographed July 5 or July 6, 1863, by Timothy H. O'Sullivan.

"What If"?

The two armies suffered between 46,000 and 51,000 casualties. Union casualties were 23,055 (3,155 killed, 14,531 wounded, 5,369 captured or missing), while Confederate casualties are more difficult to estimate.

Many authors have referred to as many as 28,000 Confederate casualties, but Busey and Martin's more recent definitive 2005 work, *Regimental Strengths and Losses*, documents 23,231 (4,708 killed, 12,693 wounded, 5,830 captured or missing) Nearly a third of Lee's general officers were killed, wounded, or captured. The casualties for both sides during the entire campaign were 57,225.

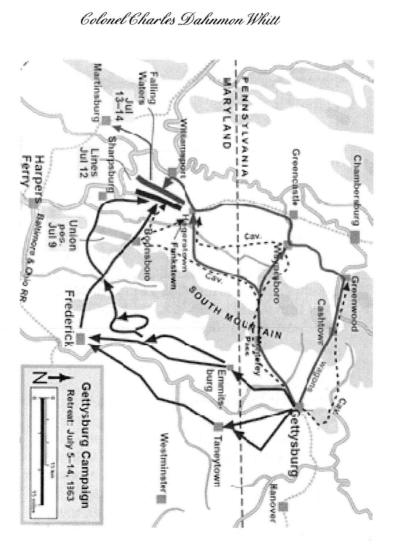

Gettysburg Campaign (July 5 – July 14, 1863).

The armies stared at one another in a heavy rain across the bloody fields on July 4, the same day that the Vicksburg garrison surrendered to Maj. Gen. Ulysses S. Grant.

Lee had reformed his lines into a defensive position on Seminary Ridge the night of July 3, evacuating the town of Gettysburg. The <u>Confederates remained on the battlefield, hoping that Meade would attack,</u> but the cautious Union commander decided against the risk, a decision for which he would later be criticized. Both armies began to collect their remaining wounded and bury some of the dead. A proposal by Lee for a prisoner exchange was rejected by Meade.

Lee started his Army of Northern Virginia in motion late the evening of July 4 towards Fairfield and Chambersburg. Cavalry under Brig. Gen. John D. Imboden was entrusted to escort the 25 mile long wagon train of supplies and wounded men that Lee wanted to take back to Virginia with him, using the route through Cashtown and Hagerstown to Williamsport, Maryland. Meade's army followed, although the pursuit was half-spirited.

(General Corse had stayed behind to guard Richmond, at hearing of Lee's retreat he took his men to meet them under force

*march. The Twenty ninth VA infantry was
part of this Army and would escort the Army
of Northern Virginia back into VA, clearing all
the gaps of Yankee soldiers.)*

The recently rain-swollen Potomac trapped
Lee's army on the north bank of the river for
a time, but when the Federals finally caught
up, the Confederates had forded the river.
The rear-guard action at Falling Waters on
July 14 added some more names to the long
casualty lists, including General Pettigrew,
who was mortally wounded.

In a brief letter to Maj. Gen. Henry W.
Halleck written on July 7, Lincoln remarked
on the two major Union victories at
Gettysburg and Vicksburg. He continued:

Now, if Gen. Meade can complete his work
so gloriously prosecuted thus far, by the
literal or substantial destruction of Lee's
army, the rebellion will be over.

The campaign continued

Halleck then relayed the contents of
Lincoln's letter to Meade in a telegram.
Despite repeated pleas from Lincoln and
Halleck, which continued over the next week,
Meade did not pursue Lee's army
aggressively enough to destroy it before it

"What If"?

crossed back over the Potomac River to safety in the South. The campaign continued into Virginia with light engagements until July 23, in the minor Battle of Manassas Gap, after which Meade abandoned any attempts at pursuit and the two armies took up positions across from each other on the Rappahannock River.

Union reaction to the news of the victory

The news of the Union victory electrified the North. A headline in *The Philadelphia Inquirer* proclaimed *"VICTORY! WATERLOO ECLIPSED!"* New York's George Templeton Strong's Direly said:

The results of this victory are priceless. ... The charm of Robert E. Lee's invincibility is broken. The Army of the Potomac has at last found a general that can handle it, and has stood nobly up to its terrible work in spite of its long disheartening list of hard-fought failures. ... Copperheads are palsied and dumb for the moment at least. ... Government is strengthened four-fold at home and abroad.

— George Templeton Strong, Diary, p. 330.

However, the Union enthusiasm soon dissipated as the public realized that Lee's army had escaped destruction and the war would continue. Lincoln complained to Secretary of the Navy Gideon Welles that *"Our army held the war in the hollow of their hand and they would not close it!"* Brig. Gen. Alexander S. Webb wrote to his father on July 17, stating that such Washington politicians as "Chase, Seward and others," disgusted with Meade, *"write to me that Lee really won that Battle!"*

Effect on the Confederacy

The Confederates had lost politically as well as militarily. During the final hours of the battle, Confederate Vice President Alexander Stephens was approaching the Union lines at Norfolk, Virginia, under a flag of truce. Although his formal instructions from Confederate President Jefferson Davis had limited his powers to negotiations on prisoner exchanges and other procedural matters, historian James M. McPherson speculates that he had informal goals of presenting peace overtures. Davis had hoped that Stephens would reach Washington from the south while Lee's victorious army was marching toward it from the north. President Lincoln, upon hearing of the Gettysburg results, refused Stephens's request to pass through the lines. Furthermore, when the news reached

"What If"?

London, any lingering hopes of European recognition of the Confederacy were finally abandoned. Henry Adams wrote, *"The disasters of the rebels are unredeemed by even any hope of success. It is now conceded that all idea of intervention is at an end."*

The immediate reaction of the Southern military and public sectors was that Gettysburg was a setback, not a disaster. The sentiment was that Lee had been successful on July 1 and had fought a valiant battle on July 2–3, but could not dislodge the Union Army from the strong defensive position to which it fled. The Confederates successfully stood their ground on July 4 and withdrew only after they realized Meade would not attack them. The withdrawal to the Potomac that could have been a disaster was handled masterfully. Furthermore, the Army of the Potomac had been kept away from Virginia farmlands for the summer and all predicted that Meade would be too timid to threaten them for the rest of the year. Lee himself had a positive view of the campaign, writing to his wife that the army had returned *"rather sooner than I had originally contemplated, but having accomplished what I proposed on leaving the Rappahannock, viz., relieving the Valley of the presence of the enemy and drawing his Army north of the*

Potomac." He was quoted as saying to Maj. John Seddon, brother of the Confederate secretary of war, *"Sir, we did whip them at Gettysburg, and it will be seen for the next six months that that army will be as quiet as a sucking dove."* Some Southern publications, such as the *Charleston Mercury*, criticized Lee's actions in the campaign and on August 8 he offered his resignation to President Davis, who quickly rejected it.

Gettysburg became a postbellum focus of the "Lost Cause", a movement by writers such as Edward A. Pollard and Jubal Early to explain the reasons for the Confederate defeat in the war. A fundamental premise of their argument was that the South was doomed because of the overwhelming advantage in manpower and industrial might possessed by the North. However, they claim it also suffered because Robert E. Lee, who up until this time had been almost invincible, was betrayed by the failures of some of his key subordinates at Gettysburg: Ewell, for failing to seize Cemetery Hill on July 1; Stuart, for depriving the army of cavalry intelligence for a key part of the campaign; and especially Longstreet, for failing to attack on July 2 as early and as forcefully as Lee had originally intended. In this view, Gettysburg was seen as a great

"What If"?

<u>lost opportunity, in which a decisive victory
by Lee could have meant the end of the war
in the Confederacy's favor.</u>

Gettysburg Address

Gettysburg National Cemetery

The ravages of war were still evident in
Gettysburg more than four months later
when, on November 19, the Soldiers'
National Cemetery was dedicated. During
this ceremony, President Abraham Lincoln
honored the fallen and redefined the purpose
of the war in his historic Gettysburg
Address.[

Today, the Gettysburg National Cemetery and Gettysburg National Military Park are maintained by the U.S. National Park Service as two of the nation's most revered historical landmarks.

Historical assessment

Decisive victory?

The nature of the result of the Battle of Gettysburg has been the subject of controversy for years. Although not seen as overwhelmingly significant at the time, particularly since the war continued for almost two years, in retrospect it has often been cited as the "turning point", usually in combination with the fall of Vicksburg the following day This is based on the hindsight that, after Gettysburg, Lee's army conducted no more strategic offensives; his army merely reacted to the initiative of Ulysses S. Grant in 1864 and 1865; and by the speculative viewpoint of the Lost Cause writers that a Confederate victory at Gettysburg might have resulted in the end of the war

The Army of the Potomac had won a victory. It might be less of a victory than Mr. Lincoln had hoped for, but it was nevertheless a victory, and, because of that, it was no longer possible for the Confederacy to win the war. The North might still lose it, to be sure, if the soldiers or the people should lose heart, but outright defeat was no longer in the cards.

Bruce Catton, *Glory Roa*

It is currently a widely held view that Gettysburg was a decisive victory for the Union, but the term is imprecise. It is inarguable that Lee's offensive on July 3 was turned back decisively and his campaign in Pennsylvania was terminated prematurely (although the Confederates at the time argued that this was a temporary setback and that the goals of the campaign were largely met). However, when the more common definition of "decisive victory" is intended; an indisputable military victory of a battle that determines or significantly influences the ultimate result of a conflict; historians are divided. For example, David J. Eicher called Gettysburg a *"strategic loss for the Confederacy"* and James M. McPherson wrote that *"Lee and his men would go on to earn further laurels. But they never again possessed the power and reputation they carried into Pennsylvania those palmy summer days of 1863."* However, Herman Hattaway and Archer Jones wrote that the *"strategic impact of the Battle of Gettysburg* was ... *fairly limited."* Steven E. Woodworth wrote that *"Gettysburg proved only the near impossibility of decisive action in the Eastern Theater."* Edwin Coddington pointed out the heavy toll on the Army of the Potomac and that *"after the battle Meade no longer possessed a truly effective instrument for the accomplishments of his task. The army needed a thorough reorganization with new commanders and fresh troops, but these changes were not made until Grant appeared on the scene in March 1864."* Joseph T. Glatthaar wrote that *"Lost opportunities and near successes plagued the Army of Northern Virginia during its Northern invasion,"* yet after Gettysburg, *"without the distractions of duty as an invading force, without the breakdown of discipline, the Army of Northern Virginia [remained] an extremely formidable force."* Ed Bearss wrote, *"Lee's invasion of the North had been a costly failure. Nevertheless, at best the Army of the Potomac had simply preserved the strategic stalemate in the Eastern Theater ..."* Peter Carmichael refers to the *"horrendous losses at Chancellorsville and Gettysburg, which effectively destroyed Lee's offensive capacity,"* implying that these cumulative losses were not the result of a single battle. Thomas Goss, writing in the U.S. Army's *Military Review* journal on the definition of

"What If"?

"decisive" and the application of that description to Gettysburg, concludes: *"For all that was decided and accomplished, the Battle of Gettysburg fails to earn the label 'decisive battle'."*

(Even with great victories, Lee lost men he could not afford.")

Lee vs. Meade

Prior to Gettysburg, Robert E. Lee had established a reputation as an almost invincible general, achieving stunning victories against superior numbers; although usually at the cost of high casualties to his army; during the Seven Days, the Northern Virginia Campaign (including the Second Battle of Bull Run), Fredericksburg, and Chancellorsville. Only the Maryland Campaign, with its tactically inconclusive Battle of Antietam, had been less than successful. Therefore, historians have attempted to explain how Lee's winning streak was interrupted so dramatically at Gettysburg. Although the issue is tainted by attempts to portray history and Lee's reputation in a manner supporting different partisan goals, the major factors in Lee's loss arguably can be attributed to:

(1) Lee's overconfidence in the invincibility of his men;

(2) the performance of his subordinates, and his management thereof;

 (3) health issues, and;

(4) the performance of his opponent, George G. Meade, and the Army of the Potomac.

Throughout the campaign, Lee was influenced by the belief that his men were invincible; most of Lee's experiences with the Army of Northern Virginia had convinced him of this, including the great victory at Chancellorsville in early May and the rout of the Union troops at Gettysburg on July 1.

Since morale plays an important role in military victory when other factors are equal, Lee did not want to dampen his army's desire to fight and resisted suggestions, principally by Longstreet, to withdraw from the recently captured Gettysburg to select a ground more favorable to his army.

War correspondent Peter W. Alexander wrote that Lee *"acted, probably, under the impression that his troops were able to carry any position however formidable. If such was the case, he committed an error, such*

"What If"?

however as the ablest commanders will sometimes fall into." Lee himself concurred with this judgment, writing to President Davis, *"No blame can be attached to the army for its failure to accomplish what was projected by me, nor should it be censured for the unreasonable expectations of the public—I am alone to blame, in perhaps expecting too much of its prowess and valor."*

The most controversial assessments of the battle involve the performance of Lee's subordinates. The dominant theme of the Lost Cause writers and many other historians is that Lee's senior generals failed him in crucial ways, directly causing the loss of the battle; the alternative viewpoint is that Lee did not manage his subordinates adequately, and did not thereby compensate for their shortcomings, Two of his corps commanders—Richard S. Ewell and A.P. Hill—had only recently been promoted and were not fully accustomed to Lee's style of command, in which he provided only general objectives and guidance to their former commander, Stonewall Jackson; Jackson translated these into detailed, specific orders to his division commanders. All four of Lee's principal commanders received criticism during the campaign and battle:

- James Longstreet suffered most severely from the wrath of the Lost Cause authors, not the least because he directly criticized Lee in postbellum writings and became a Republican after the war. His critics accuse him of attacking much later than Lee intended on July 2, squandering a chance to hit the Union Army before its defensive positions had firmed up. They also question his lack of motivation to attack strongly on July 2 and July 3 because he had argued that the army should have maneuvered to a place where it would force Meade to attack them. The alternative view is that Lee was in close contact with Longstreet during the battle, agreed to delays on the morning of July 2, and never criticized Longstreet's performance. (There is also considerable speculation about what an attack might have looked like before Dan Sickles moved the III Corps toward the Peach Orchard.)
- J.E.B. Stuart deprived Lee of cavalry intelligence during a good part of the campaign by taking his three best brigades on a path away from the army. General Lee was without eyes as to troop movements.

"What If"?

- Hooker's vigorous pursuit; the meeting engagement on July 1 that escalated into the full battle prematurely; and it also prevented Lee from understanding the full disposition of the enemy on July 2. The disagreements regarding Stuart's culpability for the situation center around the relatively vague orders issued by Lee, but most modern historians agree that both generals were responsible to some extent for the failure of the cavalry's mission early in the campaign.
- Richard S. Ewell has been universally criticized for failing to seize the high ground on the afternoon of July 1. Once again the disagreement centers on Lee's orders, which provided general guidance for Ewell to act "if practicable." Many historians speculate that Stonewall Jackson, if he had survived Chancellorsville, would have aggressively seized Culp's Hill, rendering Cemetery Hill indefensible, and changing the entire complexion of the battle. A differently worded order from Lee may have made the difference with this subordinate.
- A.P. Hill has received some criticism for his orders not to bring on a general engagement (although historians point out that Hill kept Lee well informed of his

actions during the day). However, illness minimized his personal involvement in the remainder of the battle, and Lee took the explicit step of removing troops from Hill's corps and giving them to Longstreet for Pickett's Charge.

In addition to Hill's illness, Lee's performance was affected by his own illness, which has been speculated as chest pains due to angina. He wrote to Jefferson Davis that his physical condition prevented him from offering full supervision in the field, and said, *"I am so dull that in making use of the eyes of others I am frequently misled."*

As a final factor, Lee faced a new and formidable opponent in George G. Meade, and the Army of the Potomac fought well on its home territory. Although new to his army command, Meade deployed his forces relatively effectively; relied on strong subordinates such as Winfield S. Hancock to make decisions where and when they were needed; took great advantage of defensive positions; nimbly shifted defensive resources on interior lines to make strong threats; and, unlike some of his predecessors, stood his ground throughout the battle in the face of fierce Confederate attacks. Lee was quoted before the battle as saying Meade *"would commit no blunders on my front and if I*

"What If"?

make one ... will make haste to take advantage of it." That prediction proved to be correct at Gettysburg. Stephen Sears wrote, *"The fact of the matter is that George G. Meade, unexpectedly and against all odds, thoroughly outgeneraled Robert E. Lee at Gettysburg."* Edwin B. Coddington wrote that the soldiers of the Army of the Potomac received a *"sense of triumph which grew into an imperishable faith in [themselves]. The men knew what they could do under an extremely competent general; one of lesser ability and courage could well have lost the battle."*

Meade had his own detractors as well. Similar to the situation with Lee, Meade suffered partisan attacks about his performance at Gettysburg, but he had the misfortune of experiencing them in person. Supporters of his predecessor, Maj. Gen. Joseph Hooker, lambasted Meade before the U.S. Congress's Joint Committee on the Conduct of the War, where Radical Republicans suspected that Meade was a Copperhead and tried in vain to relieve him from command. Daniel E. Sickles and Daniel Butterfield accused Meade of planning to retreat from Gettysburg during the battle. Most politicians, including Lincoln, criticized Meade for what they considered to be his tepid pursuit of Lee after the battle. A

number of Meade's most competent
subordinates—Winfield S. Hancock, John
Gibbon, Gouverneur K. Warren, and Henry
J. Hunt, all heroes of the battle, defended
Meade in print, but Meade was embittered
by the overall experience

Now What if? The second What if?
"The South Won the War at Gettysburg?"

Things could have been different on day one and also on day two, but the decision General Lee made on day three was wrong.

Lee's most trusted General, Longstreet, was talking to him about changing his mind, but he would not listen.

What really happened!

Longstreet's third division, Pickett's, arrived on the afternoon of July 2, the only division in the army which had not yet been engaged. After the day's fighting ended, Lee and Longstreet did not meet; Longstreet said he was not up to the long ride to headquarters-- so Lee sent Longstreet an order to renew his attack at daylight the next morning, throwing in Pickett's fresh division.

Next morning, however, at the hour when the attack was supposed to have started, Lee rode to Longstreet's headquarters to find his subordinate still trying to figure out how to work his way around the Union left. Pickett was not yet even in position. Lee had to scrap his original plan and make a new one. Lee and Longstreet rode up Seminary Ridge and examined the Union line on the parallel ridge to the east. Lee pointed to the Clump of Trees and designated it as the target of the day's attack. Longstreet objected--how many men were to be in the attacking force? Lee gave the figure at 15,000. Longstreet replied, *"I have been a soldier, I may say, from the ranks up to the position I now hold. I have been in pretty much all kinds of skirmishes, from those of two or three soldiers up to those of an army corps, and I think I can safely say there never was a body of fifteen thousand men who could make that attack successfully."*

Lee would not change his plan, however. In the new scheme, Hood's and McLaws's divisions would not make the initial assault. Longstreet would instead attack the Union center with Pickett's division, Heth's (now under Brig. Gen. Johnston Pettigrew) and half of Pender's (now under Maj. Gen. Isaac Trimble), plus half of Anderson's in support. <u>Longstreet balked again at such a ham-handed frontal attack, and even tried to transfer responsibility for ordering the attack onto his artillery chief, Colonel E.P. Alexander.</u> He finally resigned himself to Lee's plan, however, and personally directed

"What If"?

Pickett's men into their positions for the assault. He supervised the placement of Hill's attacking divisions less carefully. Then Longstreet wrote to Alexander: *"Colonel: Let the batteries open."*

During this bombardment, which drew a furious response from the Union guns on the ridge opposite, Longstreet showed himself at his most fearless. With the shells screaming and exploding all around him, he was observed by Brig. Gen. J.L. Kemper of Pickett's division: *"Longstreet rode slowly and alone immediately in front of our entire line. He sat his large charger with a magnificent grace and composure I never before beheld. His bearing was to me the grandest moral spectacle of the war. I expected to see him fall every instant. Still he moved on, slowly and majestically, with an inspiring confidence, composure, self-possession and repressed power in every movement and look, which fascinated me."*

Nearly two hours later, when the bombardment ended, Longstreet still could not bring himself to give the order to attack-- Pickett had to ask, *"General, shall I advance?"* and Longstreet merely nodded. "Pickett's Charge" then went to its tragic end while Longstreet watched helplessly from Seminary Ridge. Longstreet reacted quickly after the disaster by getting artillery ready to repulse a possible Union counterattack, pulling McLaws's and Hood's divisions back to a position west of the Emmitsburg Road, and helping to rally Pickett's men.

What <u>could</u> have happened?

General Longstreet knew what would result from such an assault.

"Sir", said Longstreet to General Lee, "Instead of taking a chance with this, Please consider another plan that I thought about all night."

General Lee looked at General Longstreet for a long moment, and then began to speak.

"General, we have to decide something quick," answered the Old General.

Longstreet had his attention, so he began to lay out a plan.

"Sir, we have General Stuart back with us, let's just sit back today and make plans for a forced march straight to Washington or at least to a better ground, to fight on."

General Lee stood there listening intently.

"If those people attack today, we will stand and fight, but if not, the men can get some rest and the Lord knows our animals need a breather," explained Longstreet.

General Lee called for a map to be brought forward so he could look at the feasibility of the plan.

After Lee looked at the map for a couple of minutes he looked across the little table at Longstreet with his eyebrows raised.

"Sir, I think you may be on to a plan that just might work, Meade will sit on his haunches all day wondering when we are coming; we can plan today and tonight we can move quickly," said General Lee.

"Sir, I suggest that we get our supply wagons heading towards Washington today, also we can move all of our men around and concentrate them behind us, and of course we can leave just enough men to demonstrate before the enemy, and if we do it right they will never know what we are up to," said Longstreet.

General Lee smiled at Longstreet with approval.

"When it gets dark tonight we can build our campfire's and head to better ground, I will have General Stuart's Calvary demonstrate behind their lines, and we will be twenty five miles away from them," explained General Lee.

"Yes Sir, we will have to be real careful and explain to each man not to make noise as they began to move to their new position," explained General Longstreet.

"General, do you believe that God has given you this plan?" asked General Lee?

"I do," replied a humble Longstreet.

I will write out the orders for each Corp and, you demonstrate lightly here, and have your men be a little noisy to keep Meade looking this way," said General Lee.

"Yes Sir, I will, to the best of my ability," said General Longstreet.

All day long the Army of Northern Virginia moved to a concentration point while leaving just enough men to make the enemy think they could be attacked at all points.

The wagon trains were moving towards much better ground while the Confederates teased the Yankees all day long. Meade was on good ground and was hoping Lee's men would attack. He was not about to move off the high ground.

The plan worked and now five days later The Army of Northern Virginia is all on high ground near Gaithersburg Maryland., within a couple of days ride of Washington City. The trap is set for Meade and those people, as Lee liked to call them.

The Confederates are placed in a semicircle and if Mead takes the bait he will be caught in a giant pincer that will destroy or capture him.

General Stuart is leading those people straight towards the mouth of the trap.

Some of the Southern boys that stayed behind to demonstrate against the Yankees were sacrificed for the better of the Southern Army. Most were captured so there is hope they will survive.

On July 8, 1863 The Union Army is on a forced march to catch Lee. That is what General Lee and Longstreet are hoping for.

Two thirds of the Union Army were in the pincers before they knew it. General Lee closed the pincers and they were caught.

The Union Calvary is just about all that was able to escape. There was nowhere to run, so many of the worn union boys threw down their weapons and held up their hands.

The whole Union Army is now captured except for a couple thousand that died under the volley from the Confederates as the great pincer was closed.

General Meade was captured and brought to General Lee.

General Lee was very formal and courteous to the Union General. He had a table set up and had everything in order so they could get down to the business at hand.

While this was going on the Confederate officers were having the Union soldiers guarded and began having them to stack arms.

General Lee pulled out a letter from President Jefferson Davis, which had been prepared before the Army of Northern Virginia left for the north.

General Meade had several of his ranking officers stand behind him during the business at hand.

General Lee gave the Union his conditions and General Meade read and signed, because he had no other choice.

1. The Confederate States of America do not require the United States to surrender, but to yield all the states the right to secede and be recognized as an Independent Nation.
2. The Confederate States of America require that all hostilities cease and that all Union troops and ships be removed from Confederate territory at once.
3. The United States will allow any State or territory to join the Confederate States of America in the future and trade between the nations will commence as soon as possible.
4. A meeting of Heads of State shall meet and work out any and all details.
5. If this is agreeable with the United States, The President must sign and at least ten other Officers must also sign as witness, this action must be done this very Day, July 8, 1863; or The Confederate Army will march at once and attack Washington City with any and all force they have.
Signed: Jefferson Davis, President, Confederate States of America.

The letter was signed by General Lee and ten officers, also to Union Officers signed and a copy was rushed by Union Calvary to President Lincoln in Washington.

Telegraphs were sent all over the South and North. The War is over and two nations share North America.

In the south, church bells begin to toll and folks beat on pots and pans to make their joyful noises.

There would be prayer meetings all of the South and the North. The South would be thanking and praising God; The North would be praying for hope and guidance.

States that had teetered on the decision of which side to join now came forward. West Virginia, Maryland, Missouri, and Kentucky would now join the Confederate States of America.

Some of the western territories that would form States will go with the United States and some would go with the Confederate States of America.

The new Capitol of the United States will be moved back to New York City and the

Confederate Capitol will remain in
Richmond, Virginia.

The News would be in broad lettered
headlines in every paper in America.

"And the South lived happily ever after"

Now for the Third, "What If."

Could General Jubal Early catch Washington City unprotected and win the war?

"If Jubal Early don't win the war, he will scare the pants off Washington!"

Jubal Anderson Early (November 3, 1816 – March 2, 1894) was a lawyer and Confederate general in the American Civil War. He served under Stonewall Jackson and then Robert E. Lee for almost the entire war, rising from regimental command to lieutenant general and the command of an infantry corps in the Army of Northern Virginia. He was the Confederate commander in key battles of the Valley Campaigns of 1864, including a daring raid to the outskirts of Washington, D.C. The articles written by him for the Southern Historical Society in the 1870s established the Lost Cause point of view as a long-lasting literary and cultural phenomenon.

"What If"?

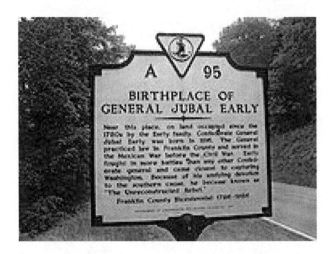

Historic marker for Jubal Early birthplace, Franklin County, Virginia

Early was born in Franklin County, Virginia, third of ten children of Ruth Hairston and Joab Early. He graduated from the United States Military Academy in 1837, ranked 18th of 50. During his tenure at the Academy he was engaged in a dispute with a fellow cadet named Lewis Addison Armistead. Armistead broke a mess plate over Early's head, an incident that prompted Armistead's resignation from the Academy.

After graduating from the Academy, Early fought against the Seminole in Florida as a second lieutenant in the 3rd U.S. Artillery regiment before resigning from the Army for the first time in 1838. He practiced law in the

1840s as a prosecutor for both Franklin and Floyd Counties in Virginia. He was noted for a case in Mississippi, where he beat the top lawyers in the state. His law practice was interrupted by the Mexican-American War from 1846–1848. He served in the Virginia House of Delegates from 1841–1843.

War of Northern Aggression

Early was a Whig and strongly opposed secession at the April 1861 Virginia convention for that purpose. However, he was soon aroused by the actions of the Federal government when President Abraham Lincoln called for 75,000 volunteers to suppress the rebellion. He accepted a commission as a brigadier general in the Virginia Militia. He was sent to Lynchburg, Virginia, to raise three regiments and then commanded one of them, the 24th Virginia Infantry, of the Confederate States Army.

Early was promoted to brigadier general after the First Battle of Bull Run (or *First Manassas*) in July 1861. In that battle, he displayed valor at Blackburn's Ford and impressed General P.G.T. Beauregard. He fought in most of the major battles in the Eastern Theater, including the Seven Days Battles, Second Bull Run, Antietam,

"What If"?

Fredericksburg, Chancellorsville, Gettysburg, and numerous battles in the Shenandoah Valley. During the Gettysburg Campaign, Early's Division occupied York, Pennsylvania, the largest Northern town to fall to the Rebels during the war.

Early was trusted and supported by Robert E. Lee, the commander of the Army of Northern Virginia. Lee affectionately called Early his *"Bad Old Man,"* because of his short temper. He appreciated Early's aggressive fighting and ability to command units independently. Most of Early's soldiers referred to him as *"Old Jube"* or *"Old Jubilee"* with enthusiasm and affection.

His subordinate generals often felt little affection. Early was a fault-finder and offered biting criticism of his subordinates at the least opportunity. He was generally blind to his own mistakes and reacted fiercely to criticism or suggestions from below.

Early was wounded at Williamsburg in 1862, while leading a charge against staggering odds.

Confederate General Jubal A. Early

Early's most important service was that summer and fall, in the Valley Campaigns of 1864, when he commanded the

"What If"?

Confederacy's last invasion of the North. As Confederate territory was rapidly being captured by the Union armies of Grant and Maj. Gen. William Tecumseh Sherman, Lee sent Early's corps to sweep Union forces from the Shenandoah Valley and to menace Washington, D.C., hoping to compel Grant to dilute his forces against Lee around Richmond and Petersburg, Virginia.

Early delayed his march for several days in a futile attempt to capture a small force under Franz Sigel at Maryland Heights near Harpers Ferry. He rested his men from July 4 through July 6. Although elements of his army would eventually reach the outskirts of Washington at a time when it was largely undefended, his delay at Maryland Heights prevented him from being able to attack the capital.

During the time of Early's Maryland Heights campaign, Grant sent two VI Corps divisions from the Army of the Potomac to reinforce Union Maj. Gen. Lew Wallace. With 5,800 men, he delayed Early for an entire day at the Battle of Monocacy, allowing more Union troops to arrive in Washington and strengthen its defenses. Early's invasion caused considerable panic in Washington and Baltimore, and he was able to get to the outskirts of Washington. He sent some cavalry under Brig. Gen. John McCausland to the west side of Washington.

Knowing that he did not have sufficient strength to capture the city, Early led skirmishes at Fort Stevens and Fort DeRussy. The opposing forces also had artillery duels on July 11 and July 12. Abraham Lincoln watched the fighting on both days from the parapet at Fort Stevens, his lanky frame a clear target for hostile military fire. After Early withdrew, he said to one of his officers, *"Major, we haven't taken Washington, but we scared Abe Lincoln like hell."*

Early crossed the Potomac into Leesburg, Virginia, on July 13 and then withdrew to the Valley. He defeated the Union army under Brig. Gen. George Crook at Kernstown on July 24, 1864. Six days later, he ordered his cavalry to burn the city of Chambersburg, Pennsylvania, in retaliation for Maj. Gen. David Hunter's burning of the homes of several prominent Southern sympathizers in Jefferson County, West Virginia earlier that month. Through early August, Early's cavalry and guerrilla forces attacked the B&O Railroad in various places.

Realizing Early could easily attack Washington, Grant sent out an army under

Maj. Gen. Philip Sheridan to subdue his forces. At times outnumbering the Confederates three to one, Sheridan defeated Early in three battles, starting in early August, and laid waste to much of the agricultural properties in the Valley. He ensured they could not supply Lee's army.

In a brilliant surprise attack, Early initially routed two thirds of the Union army at the Battle of Cedar Creek on October 19, 1864. In his post-battle dispatch to Lee, Early claimed that his troops were hungry and exhausted and fell out of their ranks to pillage the Union camp. This allowed Sheridan critical time to rally his demoralized troops and turn their morning defeat into victory over the Confederate Army that afternoon. One of Early's key subordinates, Maj. Gen. John B. Gordon, in his 1904 memoirs, attested that it was Early's decision to halt the attack for six hours in the early afternoon, and not disorganization in the ranks, that led to the rout that took place in the afternoon.

Most of the men of Early's corps rejoined Lee at Petersburg in December, while Early remained in the Valley to command a skeleton force. When his force was nearly destroyed at Waynesboro in March 1865, Early barely escaped capture with a few members of his staff. Lee relieved Early of his command soon after the encounter, because he doubted Early's ability to inspire confidence in the men he would have to recruit to continue operations.

General Lee wrote to Early of the difficulty of this decision:

While my own confidence in your ability, zeal, and devotion to the cause is unimpaired, I have nevertheless felt that I could not oppose what seems to be the current of opinion, without injustice to your reputation and injury to the service. I therefore felt constrained to endeavor to find a commander who would be more likely to develop the strength and resources of the country, and inspire the soldiers with confidence. ... Thank you for the fidelity and energy with which you have always supported my efforts and for the courage and devotion you have ever manifested in the service...

Robert E. Lee, letter to Early

General Early, disguised as a farmer, while escaping to Mexico, 1865.

Early in his elder years.

After the War

When the Army of Northern Virginia surrendered on April 9, 1865, Early escaped to Texas by horseback, where he hoped to

"What If"?

find a Confederate force still holding out. He proceeded to Mexico, and from there, sailed to Cuba and Canada. Living in Toronto, he wrote his memoir, *A Memoir of the Last Year of the War for Independence, in the Confederate States of America*, which focused on his Valley Campaign. The book was published in 1867.

Early was pardoned in 1868 by President Andrew Johnson, but still remained an unreconstructed rebel. In 1869, he returned to Virginia and resumed the practice of law. He was among the most vocal of those who promoted the Lost Cause movement. He criticized the actions of Lt. Gen. James Longstreet at Gettysburg. Together with former General P.G.T. Beauregard, Early was involved with the Louisiana Lottery.

At the age of 77, after falling down a flight of stairs, Early died in Lynchburg, Virginia. He was buried in the local Spring Hill Cemetery.

Tablet honoring Jubal Early, Rocky Mount, Virginia

Early's original inspiration for his views on the *Lost Cause* may have come from General Robert E. Lee. In Lee's published farewell order to the Army of Northern Virginia, the general spoke of the *"overwhelming resources and numbers"* that the Confederate army fought against. In a letter to Early, Lee requested information about enemy strengths from May 1864 to

"What If"?

April 1865, the period in which his army was engaged against Lt. Gen. Ulysses S. Grant (the Overland Campaign and the Siege of Petersburg). Lee wrote, *"My only object is to transmit, if possible, the truth to posterity, and do justice to our brave Soldiers."* Lee requested all *"statistics as regards numbers, destruction of private property by the Federal troops, &c."* because he intended to demonstrate the discrepancy in strength between the two armies. He believed it *would "be difficult to get the world to understand the odds against which we fought."* Referring to newspaper accounts that accused him of culpability in the loss, he wrote, *"I have not thought proper to notice, or even to correct misrepresentations of my words & acts. We shall have to be patient, & suffer for a while at least. ... At present the public mind is not prepared to receive the truth."* All of these were themes that Early and the Lost Cause writers would echo for decades.

Lost Cause themes were also taken up by memorial associations, such as the United Confederate Veterans and the United Daughters of the Confederacy. To some degree, this concept helped the (white) Southerners to cope with the dramatic social, political, and economic changes in the postbellum era, including Reconstruction.

Early's contributions to the Confederacy's final days were considered very significant. Some historians contend that he extended the war six to nine months because of his efforts at Washington, D.C., and in the Valley. The following quote summarizes an opinion held by his admirers:

Honest and outspoken, honorable and uncompromising, Jubal A. Early epitomized much that was the Southern Confederacy. His self-reliance, courage, sagacity, and devotion to the cause brought confidence then just as it inspires reverence now.

— James I. Robertson, Jr., Alumni Distinguished Professor of History, Virginia Tech; Member of the Board, Jubal A. Early Preservation Trust

Re-enactors

"The South Won" - 128 -

What if Jubal Early had marched straight on to Washington?

General Jubal Early had a grand opportunity to catch Washington City unprepared and un- protected.

It was late July 1864 and Jubal Early had men and substance enough to go in and burn Washington City.

He had lingered here and there too much and this gave General Grant time to rush troops to defend the U.S.Capital.

Lets say, Jubal Early took his men straight in to Washington and took it over.

What could Lincoln and the U.S. Government do, but to yield to the terms that General Early gave them?

President Lincoln sent telegraph messages to General Grant when Washington City fell under attack. Too late, done, done.

Washington belonged to Jubal Early and the Confederate States of America, and no number of Grants Army could help now.

"What If"?

President Lincoln sat down with Jubal Early and his officers to discuss terms.

President Lincoln kept saying, I can't sign anything; my army are on their way here to destroy you and your army.

Jubal Early spoke patiently, but with true authority, "Sir, your army is coming I'm sure, but we have you and your government; Grant will not attack us here.

"Now Mister President, I need for you to sign this letter before you, and details will be worked out later," Said General Early.

The letter was scribed out hastily by one of the Confederate officers and it said:

To the President and Government of the United States,
1 We require you to recognize the Confederate States of America as a sovereign Country.
2 You will cease all hostilities toward the southern States and the Confederate States of America. You will order your Generals to do this at once.
3. You will allow any State to join the Confederate States of America of their own free will.

4. You will remove all military, land or water from our Country, The Confederate States of America, as soon as possible.
5. If you do this we will allow you to live and let live. We will not burn this city and all that is in it if you sign now and have a number of your officials sign as witness.

A number of Congressmen were standing behind the President and they all spoke up, "Sign I,t Sir."

Many in the North were so tired of war and the killing; many protesters were in the northern cities every day protesting the war.

Vice President Johnson put his hand on Lincoln's shoulder and said, "It's time, Sir, Please sign so we can get back to our lives and the pursuit of happiness."

President Lincoln relinquished and signed the document and had a number of the Congress sign as witness.

Jubal Early extended his hand to President Lincoln, but Lincoln did not want to take it.

"Sir, we must shake on this as gentlemen to consummate it our agreement," said General Early.

What If"?

The two men shook hands and stood there
for a long minute looking at each other.

"Sir," said Jubal Early, "you must get your
telegraph messages out at once, we do not
want any more bloodshed do we?"

President Lincoln sent a message to General
Grant; *"Stop all hostilities at once, the war is*
over, make,haste to come and meet with me.
Signed: *President Abraham Lincoln.*

Jubal Early was allowed to send messages
to General Lee and to President Jefferson
Davis.

"Sir we have captured Washington and the
US Government has yielded to our
demands. Please have a guarded defensive
posture. The War is over as soon as the
word reaches all commanders, North and
South. We will hold Washington until all
signs of hostilities have ceased.
Signed: *General Jubal Early, CSA*

Jefferson Davis was interrupted in the middle
of a meeting by an aide.

"Sir," said the aide, "We have won the War."

Both the North and the South set about to stop attacks and to plan on a time of peace.

All the Confederate Army in Washington had to do was to wait for proof that General Grant had ceased all attacks against the Confederate States of America.

Two days later a scruffy and belligerent General Grant rode into Washington City. He went straight to the White House to see President Lincoln.

He was taken in to see a depressed and yet relieved, Abraham Lincoln.

"Sir, In a few more months we will beat the secessionist, what have you done?" asked General Grant?

"It is time for a new season, we must get on with the care of the United States, and let our neighbors to the south do the same," said Lincoln.

"But Sir, we can still win," said Grant.

"I have given my word and it is done, now I want you to oversee the withdrawal of all of our Army and Navy from the Confederate States in a peaceful manner," said Lincoln as

he realized this was the first time he spoke out loud, "Confederate States."

It was really over, General Jubal Early and his rag tag army had pulled of the unthinkable, they had secured peace and the new nation, The Confederate States of America.

Jubal Early will go down in history as a Southern Hero.

Telegraphs were sent all over the South and North. The War is over and two nations share North America.

In the south, church bells begin to toll and folks beat on pots and pans to make their joyful noises.

There would be prayer meetings all of the South and the North. The South would be thanking and praising God; The North would be praying for hope and guidance.

States that had teetered on the decision of which side to join now came forward. West Virginia, Maryland, Missouri, and Kentucky would now join the Confederate States of America.

Some of the western territories that would form States will go with the United States and some would go with the Confederate States of America.

The new Capitol of the United States will be moved back to New York City and the Confederate Capitol will remain in Richmond, Virginia.

The News would be in broad lettered headlines in every paper in America.

And the South Lived happily ever after.

Enjoy other books by,
Colonel Charles Dahnmon Whitt

"The Old Colonel"

Charles Dahnmon Whitt

"The South Won" - 136 -

Books tell the story

The Old Colonel, Colonel Charles Dahnmon Whitt, is shown with his six books at the Greenup Old Fashion Days Festival. His works include; "Legacy, The Days of David Crockett Whitt;" "The Patriot, Hezekiah Whitt;" "Dahnmon's Little Stories;" "Haunts and Spirits of the Past;" "Confederate American;" and "Legacy, 2nd. Edition" All of these books are based on truth and names, dates, places, and events are accurate. The books are written in Historic-Fiction fashion, with history as a story.

http://dahnmonwhittfamily. com

c-dahnmon@roadrunner.com

CPSIA information can be obtained at www.ICGtesting.com
Printed in the USA
LVOW011037061211

258049LV00001B/4/P